Praise for *Allie's Bayou Rescue,*
Book One in the Princess in Camo Series

"*Allie's Bayou Rescue* is an awesome book to read together as mom and daughter! We love how real it was about the obstacles we face as girls—but not without a God who cares for us in our struggles, pursues us, and knows EXACTLY where we are going, AND HAS IT all under control—especially when we don't."

ELISABETH AND GRACE HASSELBECK, TV PERSONALITY AND
DAUGHTER ... AND DAUGHTERS OF THE ONE TRUE KING!!

Allie's Bayou Rescue

Other Books in the Princess in Camo Series:

Running from Reality (Book 2)

faithgirlz™

PRINCESS IN CAMO
Allie's Bayou Rescue

By Missy and Mia Robertson

With Jill Osborne

ZONDERkidz

ZONDERKIDZ

Allie's Bayou Rescue
Copyright © 2018 by Missy Robertson and Mia Robertson
Illustrations © 2018 by Mina Price

This title is also available as a Zondervan ebook.

Requests for information should be addressed to:
Zonderkidz, 3900 *Sparks Dr. SE, Grand Rapids, Michigan* 49546

ISBN 978-0-310-76247-8

Cover design: Kris Nelson
Interior design: Denise Froehlich

Printed in the United States of America

17 18 19 20 21 22 23 24 25 /LSC/ 14 13 12 11 10 9 8 7 6 5 4 3 2 1

To my amazing children, nieces, and nephews
… May you never take for granted the real-
life adventures God has blessed our family with
over the last few years. Dream big, look to Him
as your trail guide, and enjoy the journey!

—Mom (Aunt Missy)

To my cousins—thank you for making
every day an adventure. I love y'all!

—Mia

CHAPTER 1

Change-up

A llie, we need to talk. Some things are about to change around here!"

Mom pulled a stool out from our kitchen island and patted the red plaid cushion for me to come and sit down. But hearing the word "change" stirred up my stomach and made me feel more like throwing up. Or doing a triple-backflip. Sometimes, when I get real nervous, I triple-flip and then throw up.

But Mom was smiling, so this had to be a *good* change, right?

I edged my way to the stool, and tried to think about the very best change that could possibly happen to me.

"Did my latest allergy tests come back? Can I eat nuts now without having my tongue swell up to the size of a bullfrog?" That would be awesome. Just to have one "death food" off my list of, well . . . too many.

Mom put her hand on my shoulder.

"No, honey, you're still allergic. The tests did come back, though, and we might have found what's causing your asthma attacks."

Panic shot from my stomach to my throat.

Please don't say pasta. Please don't say pasta. Please don't say pasta.

Mom scrunched up her nose.

"It looks like mold's a suspect."

"Mold?" I threw my hands up in the air. "That's just great. We live in Floodsville, USA."

"Yes, I know. And we'll have to work something out about that. But don't you worry about it at all. For now, let's talk about the *big* news of the day."

"Wait. Are you telling me that the big news of the day is *bigger* than finding out that living in Louisiana could kill me at any moment?"

Mom pulled out a stool and sat down. "Well, when you put it like that, no. But Louisiana is *not* going to kill you. We'll work it out, you'll see."

I hopped up on the stool next to her, swallowed hard, and gripped the cushion to hold on tight.

You can handle this, Allie. Whatever it is.

I took a deep breath and blew it out.

"Okay, give me the news. I'm ready."

Mom's blue eyes popped open wider than usual, and she slapped the counter.

"You're getting a new cousin!"

Another cousin? Well, that didn't seem like huge news at all. My dad has three brothers who are married to women who tend to have babies from time to time.

Mold seemed to be a bigger deal. But I pretended to go along with the excitement anyway.

"Who's pregnant this time? Aunt Janie?"

Mom shook her head.

"Aunt Kassie?"

"No."

"Well, Aunt Lorraine's a little older, but that would make for an interesting TV episode."

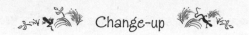

"Allie!"

"I'm just saying . . ."

My whole family stars in a reality TV show called *Carried Away with the Carroways*. For some reason, millions of people are interested in how all my uncles, aunts, grandparents, and cousins live in the Louisiana Bayou. I have a hard time understanding the fascination, because it's just something I've always known. And to be honest, I think we can be a little boring at times. Most days are spent filming what's going on around here—just us, living out our regular lives. It's kinda nuts. But at least not the kind of nuts that will cause me to stop breathing.

Mom leaned in close to me, and pushed my long, dark-blonde hair back behind one ear.

"Allie, nobody's pregnant. Kassie and Wayne are adopting Hunter!"

Now, if we had been filming a Carroway TV episode at that very moment—this is where the editors would have added the "dun, dun, dun," music into the scene.

Hunter . . . *is going to become a Carroway?*

Hunter?

Mom nudged my shoulder.

"Allie, isn't that exciting?"

I held onto that cushion with all my might to keep from bolting.

"Um . . . yes, ma'am." I tried not to make eye contact, but Mom wasn't having it.

"Well, you don't look too excited." She reached over and pulled down on my cheek with her thumb. "And your eyes are all glazed over. What did you eat for lunch?"

I shrugged.

11

"Mac and cheese." It's a good thing I'm not allergic to dairy or wheat, or I'd starve to death.

"Then why do you look so pale?" Mom put her hand on my forehead and scrunched her eyebrows together. "How's your breathing?"

I breathed in, held it, and then blew out. I wondered for a moment if this mold issue could get me out of filming TV episodes in the swamp.

"I'm good," I said, but I'm sure my fidgeting was giving me away. "Just trying to process the news."

Mom pulled her hand back and tilted her head to the side. One eyebrow shot up a little.

"Hey, I know you don't love change. And I know that Hunter can be a little rowdy at times."

"That's not a problem. Kendall's way rowdier than Hunter."

Kendall is my thirteen-year-old cousin who always sings at the top of her lungs. She's the daughter of Kassie and Wayne, so after the adoption, that would make her Hunter's sister. And *that* would make for a loud household.

Mom continued. "And I know he can be messy."

"Nope, Lola's got him beat. Have you ever seen her room? You could hide Ruby's entire preschool Sunday school class in her clothes piles."

Lola and Ruby are also my cousins, ages eleven and ten. They're the daughters of my Uncle Josiah and Aunt Janie. You'd never know they're sisters. They don't look a thing alike and their personalities are the exact opposite.

"Okay then." Mom laughed a little. "I will admit, Hunter goes a little overboard in his collecting of reptiles for pets."

I crossed my arms *and* rolled my eyes.

"Mom, reptiles *swarm* this place. I'm glad he catches some to keep them from crawling all over me."

Mom slid off her stool, walked around the kitchen island, and opened the refrigerator door. She poured a glass of iced tea and took a sip.

"Then I don't understand, Allie. What's the problem?"

The truth is—I love Hunter. He's funny and smart, and I love his big laugh. Sometimes he uses complicated words that I have to look up. But my vocabulary grades have been improving because of it. I'd been praying for him to find a loving family ever since Kassie and Wayne took him in as a foster child a couple of months earlier.

But . . . there *was* a problem. A big one.

"Allie, I asked you a question."

Mom's eyes narrowed. She put one hand on her hip, and with the other she shook her cup, rattling the ice cubes.

I struggled to pull myself out of the twilight zone.

"I'm sorry. I'm really happy for everyone."

"Then why do you look like you just whiffed fish guts?"

"I do *not* look like that. Really, everything's fine."

I tried to slip off the stool and run away, but Mom grabbed me by the shoulder.

"Allie Kate, you will stay put until we finish this conversation." When she whips out "Allie Kate," she means business.

I scooted back up to the middle of the stool and put on my serious face.

"Yes, ma'am. What was the question again?"

"What's the problem with Hunter becoming a Carroway?"

It appeared there was no getting out of it, so I tried to explain.

"Well," I sighed. "You know how all us cousins hang out all the time?"

"Of course. You can hardly avoid it. You work together, go to school together, live within shouting distance of each other . . ."

"Yes."

I opened my left hand and spread the fingers out to count on them.

"And there's me, Kendall, Lola, and Ruby."

I ticked off all four fingers, leaving the thumb without a name.

"Yes, but you have a bunch of other cousins too."

"But they're either a lot younger or a lot older. I'm talking about the ones who are the same age. Me, Kendall, Lola, and Ruby."

I ticked my fingers again.

"Okay, yeah."

"Well, now we're getting one more in the same age group."

Mom stared down at my fingers.

"That seems perfect. It'll make a whole hand full of cousins." She laughed.

I made a fist. The fingers all folded in together, and the thumb, well—it stuck out. No matter what I did with it, it just didn't seem to fit in. And there was only one reason for it.

This was going to be a challenge.

"Mom, the problem is . . . Hunter's a boy."

CHAPTER 2

New Duck in the Blind

After my meeting with Mom, I changed into my favorite coral sweats and camp T-shirt and escaped to the middle of our park-like neighborhood to do a few mandatory backflips on the grass to blow off some steam. Then I climbed up the uneven pink-and-purple wood steps that lead to the Diva Duck Blind. A duck blind is kind of like a fort—a place where hunters hide from unsuspecting ducks. Most duck blinds are located out near the water—where ducks are—and they're also camouflaged with brown and green branches. You know, so ducks can't see them.

The Diva Duck Blind is not so "camo." It's a pink and purple treehouse where Kendall, Ruby, Lola, and I hide out when we need to escape reality TV life. The Diva Duck Blind doesn't have much to do with ducks either—except that we do have a couple of pink and purple "glitter ducks" hanging from the ceiling, and when we spot our wardrobe manager, Hannah, coming up the hill, we all "duck" in the blind so she can't find us.

I pulled the cords to raise the weather-proof awnings that cover our two open windows and took a moment to soak in the warm October sunshine. Then I plopped in the middle of my favorite turquoise beanbag chair, pulled my phone from my pocket, and typed out a group text to Kendall, Lola, and Ruby:

> People, we have a serious issue to discuss.
> Meet at one o'clock in the Diva. Be prepared
> to give your secret password. NO exceptions!

Seconds after I pressed send, Lola texted me back.

> What's wrong?

I hit my forehead with the heel of my hand. I shouldn't have made the text sound so serious. Lola would imagine us all dying of some rare disease before she got here.

Another text buzzed in. This time from Ruby.

> Oooh, fun, a meeting! Can I bring cookies?

I shook my head. These two are sisters, really? I responded back.

> Cookies? For sure! No nuts.

And I grinned and waited, knowing just what Ruby would write back.

> We're all nuts!

And then she added a bunch of those laughing-til-you-cry emojis.

I didn't expect a text back from Kendall, because her phone is usually dead from all the recording she does of herself making singing videos. She's the one who wanted to name the duck blind "Diva." We went with the name because of the alliteration, and because Kendall really is a great singer. She's not too into details though—like charging her phone—so I hoped one of the other cousins would see her and bring her to the meeting.

I checked the time on my phone. Twelve-thirty. I got up and

pulled a Bible out of a backpack that was hanging from a hook on the "Allie wall."

Lord, I need help. How do you want this meeting to go?

I opened up to where my bookmark was. Romans, 5:3 "*Not only so, but we also glory in our sufferings, because we know that suffering produces perseverance; perseverance, character; and character, hope.*"

I've only lived twelve years, but this is definitely my "life-verse." It gives me encouragement when I'm frustrated with allergy shots, allergic reactions to new foods, trips to the hospital, always catching pneumonia, carrying around an emergency allergy kit, and then—as if all that isn't enough—having to be the "kid who can't have the snack" pretty much everywhere I go.

But all my stupid allergy suffering wasn't the topic of the day. Today the topic was Hunter. I needed guidance, and God promises to give it to those who ask, so I did the only thing I could think of to do. I prayed, and then I turned the page. This is what jumped out at me: "*Don't just pretend to love others. Really love them. Hate what is wrong. Hold tightly to what is good. Love each other with genuine affection, and take delight in honoring each other.*" Romans 12:9–10

I read the verse to myself about five times. Then I read it twice out loud. I paced around the Diva for a minute, staring at the verse. Then I sat back down on the beanbag and took an honest look at our Carroway cousin clubhouse. All four of us girls had been hanging out here together for years, laughing and goofing off, sharing all our problems, crying, and even praying together. I put my Bible down, stood back up, and walked around to each wall, running my fingers over our names that we'd carved in the pink-painted wood. Each cousin has her own wall, with Bible verses carved on different-sized wood pieces and nailed in. One of the verses on my wall was from 2 Corinthians 5:17: *"Anyone who belongs to Christ has become a new person. The old life is gone, a new life has begun!"*

I nailed that to my wall the day I accepted Jesus Christ as my Lord and Savior. I was nine years old, and that same day—right after I was baptized—I accidentally took a bite of a peanut butter cookie at church and almost died. Ever since then, I've carried three things with me in a mini pink backpack wherever I go: an Epi-pen, a list of the foods that could kill me, and a smooth, blue-polished stone with "Romans 5:3" carved into it.

My dad says I've been a "character" ever since that day. I'm not sure what he exactly means by that, but I do know I'm a tougher person because of all that has happened. I call things as I see them, and I'm not afraid to stand alone in a crowd. After all, I have to stand alone in different food lines all the time.

In addition to that, I've tried to follow God's plan for me. That's a little harder, because it means taking the time to listen and then obey that voice inside that whispers things that I don't always want to hear.

Like right at that moment—in our beloved clubhouse—the voice was saying this:

"Allie, if you really want to love and honor Hunter—not just pretend to love him—then this Diva Duck Blind has got to go."

CHAPTER 3

Carroway Convention

Ruby was the first to arrive for the meeting. I knew because I smelled the cookies.

"Allie!" she yelled from the bottom of the blind. "I can't open the gate. My hands are full."

I poked my head out of the open window facing the stairs.

"What's your password?"

Ruby giggled. "Little Red."

Ruby has red hair. But not the deep red kind. It's more like a harvest orange. And since it's long and gets a little frizzy in the humid Louisiana air, Ruby always braids it in one braid and pulls it forward over her right shoulder. She's super casual, and if she wears the same blue jeans and red T-shirt a couple of days in a row, well, it's not a big deal to her. In fact, she's relaxed about everything in life. Of all the cousins, I figured she'd be the easiest one to convince that we have to get rid of the Diva.

I ran down the stairs to give Ruby a hand with the gate latch and was practically knocked down as Lola entered first—without her password.

I threw my hands up in the air and gave her my are you serious look.

"Allie, don't you think we're getting a little old for passwords?" She rolled her eyes.

"California, here I come."

That's Lola's password. She hopes to live on the beach someday in Malibu, design a clothing line, and paint sunsets when she's not playing volleyball in the sand.

Today, she had a new pink streak in her short, brunette bob.

"Did you get permission from Hannah to do that?" I reached for the streak and gave it a tug to see if it was some kind of braided-in ribbon. Hannah gets a little peeved when Lola adds permanent sparkles to her appearance.

"No, I did not get permission from Hannah, because it's only temporary." Lola shut the gate and then put her hands out to inspect her fingernails, which perfectly matched the hair streak. "Plus, in my next three scenes, I have to wear a dumb camo beanie, so no one will see my hair anyway."

We wear a lot of camo in *Carried Away with the Carroways*. None of us girls are thrilled with the outfits, but Lola gets bugged about it the most because she's the most glamorous. She's also the one who designed the Diva Duck Blind—which is why there's a lot of glitter in there.

We climbed the stairs to our hideout and scarfed cookies while we settled into our favorite chairs: me on the turquoise beanbag, Lola on the pink saucer chair, and Ruby on the crooked white rocking chair we got on clearance from Cracker Barrel.

"Did either of you see Kendall out there?"

Lola and Ruby looked at each other and shrugged.

"Maybe she's filming," Ruby said. "Mom said something about Kassie and Wayne's family being on the call sheet for this morning."

"We'll hear her when she's done." Lola laid back, wrapped

her arms around her middle, and then flipped over on her side to face me.

"Allie, can't you just tell us what's going on?" Lola asked nervously. "I've had a stomachache ever since you sent the first text. You're not moving, are you?"

Ruby's eyes got big and she stopped rocking. "Lola!"

"Well, I don't want her to move to Arizona!" Lola sat up and stared at me. All of a sudden I felt like I couldn't breathe.

"What are you talking about? Why would I move to Arizona?"

Lola kept silent—looking a bit like a pink-streaked duck decoy.

Ruby filled me in.

"We overheard our mom talking to your mom this morning out on the front porch. They mentioned your asthma and how if it gets bad enough maybe you guys would have to move to Arizona."

My whole body heated up, and I felt like I was going to lose my lunch. I crossed my arms in front of me and tried to sound practical.

"That's ridiculous, people! If my family moved, how would we do the show?"

"Good point." Ruby nodded, and she started rocking again.

Lola bit her bottom lip.

"But if you don't move, how are you going to breathe?"

"Really good point," Ruby said, and she stopped rocking again.

"I'm breathing fine. But if you keep talking about this, I just might hyperventilate. So, let's change the subject."

"Okay," Lola said. "Are you going to tell us why we're here then? Besides hiding from Hannah?"

"I can't. Not until Kendall gets here."

As if on cue, a frog—not Kendall—came flying through the large open window on the north side of the duck blind. It landed on the right side of my head, got stuck in my long wavy hair, and hung there while I squealed for about twenty seconds.

Lola held her hands out, frozen in place like a statue—a statue that was trying not to laugh. "Allie, stay calm! It's just a cute little frog!"

"But he's in my hair! I want him out!"

Ruby came to my rescue and picked the green slimy thing out of my hair. It took a minute because he was tangled in there pretty good.

When she finally freed him, she examined him a minute, and smiled. Then she popped the frog in her mouth, chewed, and swallowed! I nearly fainted.

Lola's jaw hit the floor, and then she gagged.

Ruby giggled, rubbed her belly, and stuck out her green tongue.

"It was just a lime-flavored gummi."

Even so, I was grossed out. I pulled a hair tie off my wrist, and gathered my hair up into a knot on the top of my head. Just in time for another frog to fly through the window and thump me on the ear.

"Ouch!"

Another landed on the beanbag. This one was purple, so probably grape-flavored. Then a yellow one smacked Lola on the shoulder. It was just like the plague of frogs in the Bible . . . if those frogs had been candy.

"Now, wait just one minute!" Lola yelled and we all charged over to look out the north window.

"Whoever's down there, you better stop flinging the frogs before we come and—"

"Bam! Oh yeah! I've really got this down!"

It was Hunter, wearing headphones, talking to himself as he reached down to pick another candy frog out of a big, white bucket. He placed it in his slingshot, aimed up . . . and then he saw us glaring down at him.

He pulled the headphones off and let them dangle around his neck.

"Whoa—hey! What are you girls doing up there?"

Lola threw her hands in the air.

"We're getting hit by frogs! What do you think we're doing?" Then she spiked one of them back down to the ground, toward Hunter, who dodged it.

"Oh man. I'm sorry! I thought you were filming and I wanted to practice my slingshot trajectory. I saw the open window and thought, 'Hey, I bet I can get at least one frog in there,' but then I just kept hitting the target so I couldn't stop myself. You want some more?"

"Sure," Ruby said. "See if you can hit my mouth." She opened wide, and Hunter loaded up. As he pulled back on the sling, I spotted Kendall coming up the hill behind him. Her perfectly straight, light brown, shoulder-length hair blew slightly away from her face on each side, and the sun illuminated the white stone in the middle of what looked to be another new choker around her neck.

I should have been keeping my eye on the sling. This time, Hunter's trajectory was a little off. The orange-flavored frog catapulted up and hit me right in the forehead.

"Oops! Sorry, Allie!"

24

Kendall put hands on both hips and stared up at us.

"What's goin' on here? A frog war?"

"No," Hunter said. "I was practicing my aim, and I didn't know they were up there. So it was sort of like a sneak attack for all of us."

Kendall laughed, and tucked her hair back behind one ear. "Well, what *are* y'all doin' up there?"

"We're waiting on you to have a meeting," I said. "Check your phone."

Kendall pulled her phone out of the tan-leather mini messenger bag she had slung across her body.

She looked and then threw her head back. "It's dead."

"We figured that," Ruby said.

Kendall shrugged. "Guess I'll be right up." She put her phone back in the bag and then turned to Hunter.

"They're lookin' for you to film the next scene. I'd run down to the house if I were you."

Hunter's eyes widened, and he grabbed his bucket.

"Sorry about the frogs!" he yelled, and then he looked like he was going to say something else but stopped. He frowned a little, waved goodbye, and took off over the grassy hill.

My heart sank. I could tell he wanted to come up with us. He was probably just waiting for an invitation, which would never come. And that was only natural. No boys are allowed inside the Diva Duck Blind. It's an unwritten rule. And we'd never had a reason to change it.

Until now.

CHAPTER 4

Convincing Cousins

"Doe, a deer, a female deer. Ray, a drop of golden sun."

Kendall sang her password, as usual, and then as usual, asked to sing some more.

"Would you like to hear the latest song I wrote?"

"Maybe later," I said, as I opened the gate.

"Aww, I was just gettin' warmed up!" Kendall put her hand to her throat and began singing some warm-up scales."You sound good, but we don't have time for songs. We have serious issues to discuss."

I turned to climb the stairs. Kendall put her hand on my shoulder to stop me.

"No time for songs? Oh, no! Allie, are you movin'?"

I wanted to kick something.

"Why does everybody keep saying that? I am NOT moving!"

"It's just that I overheard—"

"I think that you're *all* eavesdropping just a little bit too much these days." I turned and stomped up the stairs.

When we entered the room, Ruby's and Lola's eyes were glued on me.

"Okay, spill it," Lola said.

Kendall joined me on the turquoise beanbag, but she sat with her back straight and looked at me with a frown.

I felt like I needed to stand. I breathed in deep and let out a sigh. The breath didn't come as easily as I would have liked.

"You guys, this doesn't have anything to do with anyone moving out. It has to do with someone moving in."

"Movin' in? Where? To your house?" Kendall still sat straight and adjusted her messenger bag.

"Actually, no. Someone's moving into *your* house."

Kendall shrugged. "Who?"

"I'm talking about Hunter. Your family is adopting him."

Lola pulled her legs up and crossed them on the pink chair.

"Is *that* what you called us up here for? Allie, we've known about the adoption for a week at least."

Ruby rocked and nodded while playing with her braid.

"And I obviously know." Kendall threw her whole body back on the beanbag. "He's going to be *my* little brother. We're all switchin' rooms at my house. At least I'm movin' upstairs."

"Why am I always the last to know stuff?" I shook my head, and a chill ran up my spine as a thought hit.

Maybe I was moving, and no one was planning to tell me until the day before!

"Allie, I don't see what the serious issue is." Ruby jumped up from her rocker and grabbed another cookie. "Hunter's been around for a while now. We're all used to him. He's great—for a boy—and when he's not hitting us with frogs."

"Yeah," Lola said. "I guess if he's gonna be around permanently we'll have to put protective screens on all the Diva windows."

"Screens? Don't you girls get it? We're gonna have to make more changes to the Diva than just putting up screens."

Kendall sat back up again.

"What are you talkin' about? We're *not* makin' changes. Lola made it so beautiful. It's a perfect glitter-paradise. I feel inspired to write my life-songs here."

"Why, thank you, Kendall." Lola got up and walked around our little pink and purple room and pointed to a silver teapot-shaped clock on the main wall. "Remember when Mamaw Kat took us to the church yard sale, and we found this?"

"And we didn't have any money," Kendall chimed in, "but the ladies let us pay for it with Ruby's apple pie that she made."

"And then they let us eat it!" I plopped down on the bean-bag. "And I devoured two slices." Changing the blind was going to be a tough sell. I was having second thoughts myself.

But there was God's voice again, nudging me.

Honor Hunter. Really love him.

I stood up again. Yes, this was the right thing to do.

"Girls," I said. "I love this place. It's *our* place. You know, for the Carroway cousins. We all feel welcome here, right?"

"Well, as long as I don't forget my password," Lola said, and I picked up a little pink pillow and threw it at her.

"It feels like home," Ruby said, and she flipped her braid around in circles and glanced around at the walls.

I swallowed hard and prayed that God would help me say the next thing right.

"Okay, well . . . what about Hunter? Do you think *he'd* like it in here?"

Lola crunched her eyebrows together. "Why would Hunter want to come in *here*?"

"Because *we're* all in here. And we're all the same age. And because he's going to be a Carroway cousin now too."

Kendall smacked the beanbag. "No!" She smacked it again.

"No! He doesn't get to come in here. He's gonna be my brother. That's amazing. And he's gonna be a Carroway. Awesome. He gets my old room. Fine. But not this! Not the Diva Duck Blind. Nuh-uh. He'll mess it all up with his boy stuff."

After that tirade, we all just sat silent for a few moments, listening to Ruby's rocking chair squeak.

Finally, Lola spoke. "So, what are you proposin', Allie? You've got some sort of practical solution, right? Something we'll all love, I hope?"

Kendall was staring a laser hole in my forehead.

I cleared my throat.

"I propose we redesign the place. Change everything—the name, the decorations, the atmosphere. Maybe we can even add-on, or do something crazy, like tear it down and build something new."

Kendall muffled a sob. Ruby rocked some more. Lola took the teapot clock down from the wall, wiped some of the dust off it with her sleeve, and cradled it in her arms.

"Change is a good thing, right?" I said, trying to convince myself too.

"Maybe we should take a few days to pray about it," Kendall said.

"No." Lola put the clock back up on the wall. "That's just delaying the inevitable. We already know what God would want. Did you all see Hunter's face when he left a while ago? I could tell—he wanted us to invite him up here, and he was sad when we didn't. As much as I hate to think about changing this place . . . Allie's right."

"Lola," Ruby said, "you can make this place even cooler than

29

it is now! And we can ask Dad and Uncle Jake if they can add a room or two."

"Now just wait a minute, y'all!" Kendall was up pacing back and forth. "How do we know that Hunter will even appreciate all that we're givin' up for him? Shouldn't *he* have to do somethin'? Show that he's willin' to do whatever it takes to become a Carroway cousin? You know—*earn* his password? I don't want him just waltzin' in here, thinkin' he gets everything without givin' anything."

"Wow, you're sounding like a real big sister already," Lola said.

Ruby shrugged. "I like Kendall's idea. We could have some kind of ceremony, where he pledges to be a loyal cousin and signs a contract, something like that. We could take the pledge too."

Kendall crossed her arms in front of her. "That's too easy! I think he should have to prove his worth. By doin' things. Hard things. Things that Carroways have to do all the time."

"Are you talking about an initiation?" I was scared asking the question. Even more scared about how she might respond.

Kendall wiggled her eyebrows up and down.

"That's exactly what I'm talkin' about."

CHAPTER 5

Initiation Appreciation

Kendall's eyebrows were still doing their thing when we heard a familiar voice over the loudspeaker.

"Attention, Carroway children! This is HANNAH!"

"Oh dear," Ruby said.

The speaker continued.

"You have exactly TWENTY minutes to change into your dove hunting clothes, and report to field three for filming. That's three, ladies! ONE . . . TWO . . . THU-REE!"

"Oh dear," Ruby said again. "I don't know where my dove hunting clothes are."

Our eyes all fixed on Ruby.

"Think, Ruby," I said. "Where did you last see them?"

She put her hand over her mouth and shook her head.

"Ummmm."

"And IF YOU'RE LATE . . ."

"Hannah sounds a little stressed today," Lola said.

"I will bring my NERF GUN and HUNT YOU DOWN. And after I shoot you, I'll STUFF YOU and HANG YOU ON THE WALL IN MY LIVING ROOM!"

Ruby started jogging in place. "I better go."

Then we heard an evil giggle over the speaker.

"Y'all know she's not serious," Kendall said.

"KENDALL, that means YOU TOO!"

31

"She sure sounds serious," I said, and I put my arms out to gather everyone in for a huddle.

I threw my hand out in the middle, and the girls put their hands on top of mine. I think Ruby's was shaking a little.

"Okay," I said. "Each of you come up with one task that Hunter will have to perform during his initiation. It has to be hard. A Carroway thing. Get your idea to me by tonight. Got it?"

"Got it!" everyone said.

"Okay, Carroways on three."

We pumped our hands up and down.

"One, two, three . . ."

"CARROWAYS!"

Then we all ran down the steps of the Diva and over the hills to our individual houses to search for our dove hunting clothes. By the time I got to my house, I was breathing hard, my head felt fuzzy, and my hands shook. I noticed that the tips of my fingers were turning a little blue, but I shoved them into my pockets.

No time to think about anything right now but changing clothes.

On my way in the door, I practically ran right into a tall, skinny man dressed in a business suit. He carried a book bag and looked like a computer nerd.

"Oh, hello," he said. "Hey! You're Allie, right? I watched your show last night. The one where you brought your class duck home for the weekend, and it got away, and you were afraid your dad was going to shoot it and serve it for dinner? Hilarious!"

The man doubled over with laughter. My family has that effect on people.

I tried to be polite. I mean, as polite as I could be after finding a complete stranger in my house.

"I'm sorry, who did you say you were?"

The man stopped laughing and straightened back up.

"Oh, I'm sorry. You're probably wondering what I'm doing here in your house."

"Yes sir."

He reached in his pocket and pulled out a business card.

"Ed Castro, home appraiser. My company sent me over. Your mom said to come on in."

This happens a lot. People show up and do things in our house. Film crews, maintenance people, decorators. But something about this guy made me nervous.

I grabbed the card and looked at it.

"What exactly does a home appraiser do?"

"Oh, well, it's simple, really. An appraiser looks around a house and decides what the whole thing is worth."

"What for?"

Mr. Castro shrugged. "For lots of reasons. But mostly because a family wants to refinance or sell."

My mind stuck on the word "sell."

I frowned.

"I'm sorry," Mr. Castro said. "I'm invading your privacy. I can come back another time . . ."

I gently shook my hands out. The color was back in the tips of my fingers.

"Oh, no, you can stay. I'm sorry if I seemed rude. Go ahead, and look at the house all you want."

Then I got an idea.

"Mr. Castro, can I ask you a question?"

"Sure." He bent down and pulled a tablet out of the book bag.

"Well, I've always worried about this. As you probably know, since you watch the show, I have these two big brothers who have been wrestling in our upstairs den for years. Seriously, we're talking hours and hours, and sometimes I would be down here in the kitchen, and I would worry about the floor breaking away and them falling through. Could that happen? I mean, the floor really creaks up there now."

Mr. Castro shook his head. "You Carroways. You're such a crazy bunch." Then he looked up at the ceiling. "You're saying the den is right above here?"

"Yes, sir."

He pulled our stepstool over from the corner, climbed up on the top step, and poked the ceiling a few places.

"Seems okay," he said.

"And then there was that bathtub overflow incident."

Mr. Castro climbed back down and started laughing again. "I saw that episode too! When you and the cousins decided to give that goat a bath, right? And it got away and ran down the hall, and you left the water running . . ."

"Well, I thought Ruby was going to turn it off. I had a crazy, soaped-up goat to catch."

"Oh, I wasn't trying to make fun." Mr. Castro adjusted his glasses. "It was just so entertaining! So, are you saying *this* was the house that had the flood?"

"Yes, sir. The bathroom is right down the hall from the creaky-floor den. First door on the right."

"I'll check that."

"Good. I really want the appraisal to be fair."

"You're good, honest people."

I smiled. "Thanks."

All of a sudden, I remembered the Nerf gun, and I imagined Hannah arriving at my door at any second.

"I've gotta go. I'm running out of time. I have to go find my dove hunting clothes before I'm the one being hunted down and stuffed by our wardrobe manager."

Mr. Castro laughed again.

"Oh man, this has been the best afternoon. I can't wait to tell the people at work that I met you."

I smiled. "Tell them I said hi. And good luck checking out the house."

"Thanks. It'll be fun."

I ran toward the stairs but then turned back around.

"Mr. Castro? I forgot, there's one more problem with the house."

He scrolled on his tablet and then looked up.

"What's that?"

I put my finger to my chin and thought a minute.

"Uh, never mind. I'm sure you'll find it. It's hard to miss."

Mr. Castro pointed his finger at me and winked.

"You're one of my favorites in the show. And my family has been praying for you and all those allergies."

I grinned.

"Thanks. I really appreciate it. I'm sorry, I gotta go."

He waved.

"See you soon, Allie. If not here, then on TV."

I waved back, then hurried up the stairs. I flew into my room, threw open the closet door, and pulled out the hangers marked Dove Hunting Clothes.

It was just a black T-shirt with black pants, but Mom marks everything so there is no doubt. And I'm grateful, because I never want to get Hannah mad at me—even if she is just faking about the Nerf gun thing. At least, I'm pretty sure she is.

I pulled on the clothes and checked the clock. Five minutes left till call time. I breathed a sigh of relief. And I actually got a really good, deep breath.

Maybe Mr. Castro's family's prayers were already working, and we wouldn't have to sell our house and move to Arizona.

CHAPTER 6

Dove Love

Allie, I knew *you'd* be here on time." Hannah is sweet in person. She's petite and has the cutest short red hair, cut to make it fall every which way—a perfect bed-head style. She also looks like she wouldn't hurt a fly. But that loudspeaker does something to her. I do have to give her credit—she always scares us into being on time.

Except maybe today. I stood there, watching the time tick away on my phone, while Kendall, Ruby, and Lola all came skidding into field three—all wearing black clothes like mine. But it was five minutes past the call time, and no sign of Hunter.

"We'll wait another five minutes, and then send someone to go find him." Hannah paced back and forth, but she still wore a grin, so I guessed we were okay for now.

"Did you see him on your way over, Kendall?" Ruby fidgeted with her braid with one hand and twirled her dark-green camo beanie on her other hand.

"No, last time I saw him was the frog war."

"He's got to be around here someplace," Lola said. "I hope he's not hurt. Let's go find him, Allie."

Lola grabbed me by the elbow and pulled me forward. Hunter didn't have his own phone yet, or we could just call him. And if he were loud like the rest of the Carroway boys, we'd just have to listen for a while. But Hunter's a thinker and a little bit more quiet. He could be hiding out anywhere.

And now he was late.

I cupped my hands around my mouth and yelled, "Hunter!"

"Where would you go if you were a boy?" Lola pulled her beanie off and shook her short, dark mop. The pink streak caught the sunlight and looked pretty cool.

"Hmmm. I guess I would go somewhere I could get dirty. But I don't think Hunter likes dirt."

"Hunter!" I called again, and I scanned the horizon. Nothing.

The loudspeaker crackled to life.

"Hunter Carroway, this is HANNAH! You are LATE, buddy-boy! If you do not report in five minutes, you will be cut from the dove-hunting episode! Lola! Allie! Turn around and report to field three. That's ONE . . . TWO . . . THU-REE!"

That's when we saw him. He had his head down as he climbed up the hill from the creek. He was dressed in black and walking slow. His short, blond waves bounced on top of his head. He took his dark-framed glasses off, wiped them with his shirt, and adjusted them back on his nose. When he saw us, he stopped walking and wiped his chin with his sleeve.

"Hunter?" Lola ran over to meet him first and put her hand on his shoulder. I caught up just in time to hear what the problem was.

"I don't like hunting. There. I said it." Hunter looked up at us—his super bright green eyes clouded. His right cheek was wet. "I don't want to shoot doves."

"What?" Lola covered her mouth and looked to the sky.

"But your name's Hunter," I said. "And you live in Louisiana. With . . . our family."

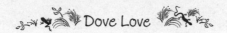

"Yes, I know. It's quite unfortunate. Not the family thing. The name thing."

"What's your middle name?" Lola asked.

"Buster."

I laughed a little.

"Nuh-uh. Hunter Buster? Really?"

Lola shook her head.

"I suppose you don't like busting things up either."

"I'm more of a builder," Hunter said.

"Well, that's admirable." I wanted to tell him right then that he could help us build the new duck blind. But first, he had to earn the privilege.

"But it does present a problem," Lola said. "Because right now you're expected to go dove hunting."

Hunter shook his head, turned, and started back down to the creek.

"Just tell them you couldn't find me. I'll be down here preparing for my punishment."

"Now you just wait a minute, Hunter Buster Builder." I grabbed Hunter by the back of his shirt and held on until he stopped walking. "We're going to help you figure something out."

"But I don't want anyone to find out. At least not today. I couldn't take the humiliation."

"Who says there has to be humiliation?" Lola said. "Everyone in this family is different. I don't particularly love hunting, you know."

Hunter grinned. "Really?"

"Sure," Lola said. "The wardrobe is horrible. Take this beanie, for instance. Messes with my hair. And dirt gets under my fingernails." She held out her fingers with a dramatic pink tone splashed on each nail. "But I do like to shoot," she said. "So maybe you just have to figure out what part of dove hunting you do like, and focus on that."

Lola always knows what to say to comfort people. It's like she can feel their sadness and knows just what to do. While she talked, she walked toward field three, and Hunter walked side-by-side with her.

"I actually really like guns," Hunter said. "The machinery and how they work fascinates me."

"And do you like to eat?" Lola almost had him all the way to Hannah.

"Yes." He was even smiling now.

"So you're not against people hunting for food, you just don't want to be the one to do it, right?"

Hunter shrugged. "I guess."

"Okay, then, here's the plan," Lola said. "When they cue you, shoot the gun up high so you're sure to miss. Act frustrated. Then when they cue me to shoot, cheer me on. I'll drop a few doves out of the sky, and we'll high-five each other. How does that sound?"

Hunter grinned. "Sounds like reality TV at its finest."

We all laughed.

"Please don't tell *anyone* what I told you about the hunting," Hunter said. "Not even Ruby and *especially* not Kendall. Promise?"

"Promise," I said, and I held up my hand like I was taking an oath.

"Promise," Lola said, and she held her hand up too. And as Hunter ran toward field three, Lola turned to me and gave me a look.

I knew right then what she was thinking.

How am I supposed to keep a secret from my sister?

CHAPTER 7

Initiation List

What to include in Hunter's initiation was the secret conversation between us girls during dove-hunting filming. Since there are lots of takes and breaks during any filming, we've invented some ways to communicate while pretending to pay attention.

One of those ways is writing in the dirt.

Between the first and second takes, we sat clustered on a dirt hill. Kendall picked up a stick and wrote.

#1. Hunt for food. Cook it.

Ruby nodded her head and clapped her hands together without making a sound.

Kendall scratched the words out just as soon as we all saw it, erasing the evidence

Then she whispered, "All Carroways have to hunt, right? And you sure can't eat raw food. So he's got to cook it."

I swallowed hard and glanced at Lola, who fidgeted and fussed with her beanie.

"That shouldn't be number one," she said. "Can't we start him off with something easy and fun? How about . . ."

Lola grabbed the stick and wrote: #1. Sing with our group.

Lola's brilliant. She hit Kendall right in the heart with that one.

Kendall grabbed the stick and drew a happy face.

41

We Carroway girls have a singing group. Kendall is the lead, of course, and she writes most of the songs. Lola, Ruby, and I are the back-up girls, but we can sing some mean harmonies. We've sung at church, in school talent shows, and recently, we've sung a little on stage when we go to speaking events with our family.

We're pretty good.

"Cut!" Zeke, our director, called for the end of the scene they were filming with Uncle Wayne a few yards away. "Girls and Hunter, your turn. Come get your guns. Hunter, yours is loaded, so stay right there with Thomas and Turbo."

Safety is a huge thing on the set of *Carried Away with the Carroways*. The only loaded gun is the one that belongs to the person who's going to pull the trigger, and if it's a kid—in this case, Hunter—then Thomas, our weapons specialist, sticks with him like chewed-up gum on a shoe. Oh, and Turbo is a Golden Retriever—he retrieves all the birds we shoot.

Hunter—like all of us—has been through several hours of gun safety training, and he's a good shot too. He destroys targets and loves it. But for this scene, he must have been shaking in his boots, since there were going to be real-live doves in front of him. I noticed him hugging Turbo's neck a bunch of times, most likely for comfort.

"On my cue," Zeke said, "you all walk forward, slowly. Girls, stay behind Hunter. Lola, mention that your beanie itches. Allie, sneeze a couple of times, okay?"

I rolled my eyes. This allergy stuff was starting to define me a little too much.

"Kendall, hum a little song. Whatever comes to mind. Ruby, stop and admire those wildflowers over there." Zeke pointed to a purple patch of hollyhocks that grow like weeds around here.

Much of what Zeke tells us to do are things we would already do, without being told. So I think it's funny that he has to cue us and give us lines to say.

"Hunter, as soon as you get close to that pack of doves, start running toward them, and when they fly, shoot away. Got it?"

Hunter nodded and gave Zeke a shaky thumbs-up. Then he turned back to look at Lola, who pointed her index finger straight up and pretended to pull a fake trigger with her thumb.

"Action!" Zeke stepped away and let the film crew move in with their cameras and microphones on wheels.

We all moved forward. I sneezed, but for real. I must have hit a mold-pocket with my boot.

Kendall hummed, and Lola shushed her while she adjusted her beanie. Ruby knelt to pick a wildflower and stuck it in her braid. I love how we add artistic touches to the show.

And all of a sudden, Hunter became Tarzan! He rushed forward, screaming a war cry. You need to really make a racket to get doves to move. His voice cracked, which was hilarious. Thomas ran forward, right behind him. The doves stirred. Hunter yelled again, and his voice cracked again. The birds finally flapped their wings and flew for their lives.

Hunter raised his rifle, a little too high, just like Lola said.

He pulled the trigger, and the shots rang out. Turbo barked and ran forward. Most of the doves flew on, safe for another day.

Except for one.

"YEAH!" The crew cheered, and a couple of them jumped up and pumped fists in the air.

It was Hunter's first TV kill.

"Cut!" Zeke ran over and slapped Hunter on the back, a huge smile on his face.

Thomas grabbed the gun from Hunter, who stood there, staring up at the sky.

I said a quick prayer that he wouldn't melt down too bad in front of everyone, especially after Uncle Wayne ran over to Turbo, got the dead dove out of his mouth, and carried it by the tail over to Hunter.

"Great job, son!" he said, and he patted Hunter on the shoulder. "You're a natural!"

Kendall came up to me and whispered, "Singing might be the hardest thing for him after all. Did you hear that voice? How are we going to work that crackle into our quartet?"

"Okay, everyone take a break! Lola, you're up next." Zeke called the film crew over and pointed in different directions. Then they were off to set up for the next Carroway kid hunting scene.

"Let's get a cold drink." Uncle Wayne put his arm around Hunter and walked him over to the refreshment tent.

Kendall pulled us girls back over to our dirt hill, and told us to sit down.

"We have to make it harder!"

"Make what harder?" Ruby asked.

"The initiation!" Kendall adjusted her camo choker. "We can't just hand over our beloved Diva. He needs to struggle a little. Be forced out of his comfort zone. Clearly hunting isn't a challenge."

Lola shifted her eyes to meet mine.

If Kendall only knew.

"C'mon girls, think!" Kendall dragged a stick through the dirt. "We need somethin' hard."

"Catching bullfrogs is hard," Ruby said. "Fun, but hard."

"And muddy." Lola scraped some dirt out from under her thumbnail.

"Hunter hates mud," I said. "Remember how he offered to help in the kitchen instead of playing in the mud pit at camp?"

Kendall grinned and wrote in the dirt: #1. Catch bullfrogs in the mud.

"It's what all true Carroways do. Great idea, Ruby."

"Okay," I said. "We have bullfrogs in the mud, sing with the quartet, hunt for food and cook it. I say that sounds like a solid initiation."

"No." Kendall shook her head. "We need one more thing. Somethin' epic."

She put her fist to her chin. "How about somethin' scary? Any true Carroway has to be able to conquer their fears."

"Really?" Ruby asked. "I don't remember ever being afraid of anything."

"What? How about snakes, hurricanes, floods, that time you got lost at Disney World . . ."

Ruby turned white listening to Lola tick off her fright list.

Then the perfect thing came to me.

"And let's not forget something every Carroway is afraid of . . ."

I leaned in and paused to let everyone focus in on my words. "Mamaw and Papaw's haunted storage shed."

They all gasped. Kendall shook her head.

"NO! He'll have a heart attack in there as soon as he hears the first groan. Plus, I don't want to lose my new brother before he's even officially adopted."

"Oh, come on, Kendall," I said, "You don't really *believe* that story, do you?"

"I do," Ruby said.

"The story's true, Allie." Lola pulled her beanie down over her ears and pushed her jacket collar up a little higher to cover her neck.

"You really believe there was a fifth brother who disappeared in that shed?"

Everyone nodded.

"A demon-possessed alligator—bent on revenge—ate Uncle Andy." Lola pulled her head into her jacket like a turtle hiding in its shell.

"While he was looking for Mamaw's Thanksgiving tablecloths." Ruby shuddered. "Which explains why Mamaw only uses placemats now."

"You people are crazy. There never was an Uncle Andy."

"Allie, I've seen pictures of him," Kendall said. "He was only twelve-years-old when it happened. It creeps me out. Hunter's twelve. What if the gator comes for him? You know, to get back at Great Uncle Rhett for runnin' over its dad with the tractor?"

"It's all a ridiculous Carroway fable," I said. "Come on! Don't you think it's odd that we only hear that story during campfires when we're eating s'mores and one of the uncles is shining a flashlight up his nose?"

"They can't tell it in the light," Lola said. "The dark hides their tears."

"But we've all been in that shed tons of times looking for

stuff for Mamaw. It's creepy, and there are some weird noises that I can't explain, but we always come out."

"That's because the gator only eats boys, remember? That's why none of the uncles go in there for anything."

"People, they just use that as an excuse because they don't want to crawl around in there and hurt their backs! Do you think they'd send us—their precious daughters—if they thought we'd get eaten by some mad alligator?"

"Like I said before," Lola popped her head out. "The gator only eats boys. Twelve-year-old Carroway boys."

"And seasonal tablecloths." Ruby hid her face in her hands.

"This. Is. Ridiculous." I crossed my arms and looked around at my cowering cousins. That family fable had sunk deep into their little fear-filled hearts.

"Well, okay then. Since each of you has suggested a task for Hunter's initiation, I think it's only fair that I submit one too."

I lifted my index finger into the air. "To pass the initiation, to be honored as a true Carroway, and in order for us to turn our lovely Diva Duck Blind into an acceptable dwelling for girls *and* a boy, our new cousin and brother Hunter must survive a whole hour in Mamaw and Papaw's haunted storage shed. In. The. Dark."

Lola pushed her beanie back to show her eyes and forehead. "And *what* if he doesn't survive?"

I shrugged. "Then I'll finally agree with you that the story of our dear-departed Uncle Andy and the Gruesome Gator is true."

I gave them my most evil Halloween laugh, but nobody seemed to appreciate it.

Lola whimpered. Kendall stared at me like I was some kind

of criminal. Ruby wouldn't take her eyes off the ground and just flicked her red braid back and forth.

"What's going on, ladies?"

We all jumped about a mile.

"Did you see my shot? Boy, that was a surprise! Got it on my first try." Hunter shook his head. His hands appeared to shake a little too. "This year has been full of surprises."

"There's more to come," Kendall said.

"Oh, yeah? You know something I don't?"

Lola stood up and brushed off her pants. "I say we tell him now."

Ruby came back to life and stood too. "It's only fair."

Kendall drew her hand across her throat to signal us to stop the conversation.

"But we haven't agreed to all—"

"Yes, we have," I said. "It's been decided. Hunter just has to agree."

"Agree? To what?"

CHAPTER 8

All In

Hannah pounced on us before we got a chance to clue Hunter in on his initiation.

"Zeke decided one dead dove is enough for today. He wants to film the dinner scene. So you know what that means, ladies and gentleman?"

"We have to change clothes?" Hunter pushed his glasses up on his nose as he looked up at Hannah. He seemed relieved.

Hannah smiled and gave him a side hug. "You are quickly becoming my favorite, you know that? Yes, it's time for a wardrobe adjustment." She looked down at the big white sports watch on her wrist. "Call time is four o'clock, so y'all have two hours to make yourselves presentable for dinner."

Lola sighed. "Good. I have to fix this flattened hair." She popped the beanie off her head, and Hannah cringed and pointed to the pink streak.

"What is THAT?"

"Oops." Lola tried to shove the beanie back on but Hannah grabbed it from her.

"Tell me that's a feather. Or a ribbon. Tell me that you did not dye your hair."

"It's temporary! Plus, the next three scenes were supposed to be in a beanie. Can I help it if Zeke changes his mind?"

"Fine." Hannah threw her hands in the air. "Then you can

49

explain to the crew why they can only film the left side of your head."

And she stomped off.

Then she turned around. "Four o'clock at Maggie and Jake's! Allie-girl, you better go clean up the clutter on your dining room table!"

My mind flashed to our dining room, and the big round table that catches everything—homework, TV scripts, bills, empty cups . . . you name it, it's on that table.

"I better go." I took my foot and brushed it over all our writing scribbles in the dirt, destroying all the evidence.

Hunter put his arm out.

"You can't go yet. You were about to tell me about my surprise."

The girls and I all looked at each other.

"Okay, gather in." I put my arms out to pull everyone in. When they were all close, I spoke low.

"We have time, but we can't do it here. We'll tell you all about your surprise up in the duck blind in exactly ten minutes."

Hunter stepped back. "The Diva? I'm allowed up there?"

Kendall cleared her throat.

"No, you are not. But for today, and today only, we will issue you a temporary password."

"Do I get to pick it?"

"No," I said. "You will find your temporary password written on a pink post-it note and shoved in the magenta mailbox at the base of the blind. When you retrieve the password, you must knock on the gate four times and wait for one of us to come down to meet you. Whisper the password into that person's ear, and then eat the post-it note."

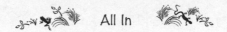

Ruby chuckled a little at that.

"What?" Hunter's voice cracked. "You want me to eat paper?"

Lola and Kendall giggled.

"Nah, I was just kidding. But you *must* flush it down the toilet at your earliest convenience. Got it? We don't mess with passwords around here. If someone finds it and uses it, we'll lose all control."

"She's not kiddin'," Kendall said.

Now I was trying not to laugh.

Hunter stood up straight and saluted us.

"I will do my best to comply. See you in ten minutes at the duck blind."

Then he zoomed down the hill, disappearing in seconds.

"Ten minutes?" Kendall said, and she gave me a funny look.

"Yeah. It's just enough time for us to get there and figure out a password."

"And I hope we're not out of pink post-its," Ruby said.

"Not a chance," Lola said. "What shade do you want? Pale? Deep magenta? I stocked a new batch just last week."

We arrived at the blind with six minutes to spare. On the way over, I chose the password. It was a simple one—Gator Buster. Oh, how I wanted our new cousin, Hunter Buster, to bust that silly gator story to bits!

I scribbled the password on the post-it and ran down the Diva stairs to stuff it in the mailbox. Inside, I was surprised to find an old post-it with the words "Diva Dad" on it. Though the Diva is off limits to boys, sometimes we let our dads in, mostly to do repairs. But the time I gave my dad this password he had come up to help me write an essay about flood control on the Ouachita River, which is near where we live. I would have to talk to him later about his careless handling of temporary passwords.

Eat it or flush it. Those are the *only* two options.

The girls peppered me with questions as soon as I got back up the steps of the blind.

"What exactly are you going to tell Hunter?" Lola fiddled with her hair, trying to hide the streak.

"When are we going to do the initiation?" Kendall paced back and forth.

"What are we going to tell our parents?" Ruby rocked away on her crooked chair.

"What if Hunter says no?" Lola jumped in again.

I held both hands out.

"People! Why are you so worried? This is a *fun* thing, remember? We're not doing anything bad, and we're not going to lie to anyone. We're just going to do what all Carroways do! It'll all work out. You'll see. We'll simply ask Mamaw if we can all come out to her house to spend the night." I plopped down on the turquoise beanbag and leaned my head on one of the Scripture boards. I tried to picture what our duck blind would look like when we included Hunter's decorating tastes in the new design.

"That's a good plan." Ruby smiled. "Mamaw *always* says yes."

Just then, we heard four loud knocks. And for some reason—all of a sudden—I was a little dizzy. I sat up straight and tried to take a deep breath, but it felt like I had a brick laying on my chest. I had to settle for a few shallow breaths and tingly fingers.

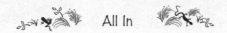

"Ruby," I squeaked out. "Can you go down and retrieve Hunter?"

"Sure." She popped out of her rocker and vanished down the steps.

Part of me wanted to go down there and watch the beginning of this little adventure. But I had no air at the moment, so I stayed put.

Ruby and Hunter appeared in seconds. Ruby situated herself back on the rocker, and Hunter just stood there, staring wide-eyed as he took in the blind.

"What planet is *this*?" he said, and he began to walk around, picking up and inspecting some of our fragile collectables.

"Hey—be careful with that," Kendall said, and she rushed over to save her souvenir glass giraffe that she had bought at the zoo. She took it from Hunter and gently placed it back on the white teacart that Mamaw Kat got for us at the flea market.

Hunter immediately picked up a red teacup and saucer, a gift I had given Ruby for her tenth birthday.

Ruby stopped rocking and watched in horror while Hunter lifted his pinkie finger and pretended to drink out of it. Then he gulped, burped, and placed the teacup back down on the cart.

"Lovely afternoon for tea," he said. Then he spotted the glittered duck decoys hanging from the ceiling.

"How could you do *that* to those poor ducks?" He pointed up. "Why the ribbon and beads?" He stepped closer to inspect. "Are those duck calls?" He poked the turquoise, purple, and pink tubes hanging from the ribbon that we made to look like duck calls. Then he pointed to me.

"Does your *dad* know you did this to perfectly good duck decoys?"

I nodded. "Yes. He wasn't happy about it."

Hunter swept his hands around the room.

"Well, why would *any* boy ever want to visit a place like *this*? I can't believe I've felt sad about being excluded for the last few weeks."

I swallowed hard and tried to take another deep breath.

"We didn't mean to leave you out, Hunter." Ruby got up and offered him a cookie from earlier. "We just never thought about it. It's always been the place where we girls hang out."

"Yeah, we're really sorry," Lola said.

Hunter accepted the cookie, took a huge bite, and talked while he chewed.

"It's okay. I know I'm an outsider. Clearly I don't fit in here anyway."

"Yes, you do!" Air filled my head, but somehow not much of it made it to my lungs.

"Huh?" Hunter downed the rest of his cookie, brushed the crumbs off his hands, and sat down cross-legged on the floor.

"Well, I mean—we've been discussing making some changes to the place."

"I hope you're going to add some camo. I mean, what's a Carroway clubhouse without camo?"

"Puh-lease," Lola said. "Isn't it enough that we have to wear it for filming all the time?"

Kendall, who had been inspecting her precious giraffe for damage, finally piped up.

"Hold on a minute. We've only been *discussing* changes. It doesn't mean we're gonna make 'em." She turned toward Hunter and crossed her arms in front of her. "It all depends on you, Brother."

"Me?" Hunter pointed both thumbs at his chest. "What do I have to do with it?"

I stood and tried to sound formal.

"Hunter, we're all very excited that you're officially joining the Carroway family. But the whole legal thing is about to get *very boring*—you know, with trips to the courthouse, having to dress up, waiting around while people sign papers, the never-ending picture taking, relatives crying and hugging, the formal announcements . . ."

"Wow, I never thought about that as being boring, but you have a point."

"So we thought we should add a little fun to the whole thing. Just for us cousins."

"What do you have in mind?"

Kendall butted in.

"An initiation. You see, Hunter, there are things that make up a true Carroway, and we want you to be prepared. Because we care. So, we created a list of things that you will need to do to pass."

"To *pass*? Wait. What if I don't pass? Do you kick me out of the family?"

"No, silly," I said. "But if you *do* pass, we have a surprise for you. As a tribute to you, our new brother and cousin, we will redesign the Diva Duck Blind. And we'll all get to hang out here together."

"Will I get a permanent password?"

"Yep," Kendall said. "And you can choose what it is."

Hunter closed his eyes. He shook his head like he was trying to clear his mind of all things glitter. He sat there for a minute.

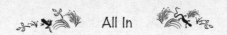

There was silence in the blind for at least thirty seconds. Then Hunter shot to his feet.

"I'm ALL IN, ladies! When do I start?"

I grabbed my chest. My immediate thought was, As *soon as I can breathe*.

CHAPTER 9

Clearing the Air

I exhaled hard, and a weird whistling sound came out of my throat. Or was it my chest?

"Allie! You look like a ghost!" Hunter lunged over to me and pushed down on my shoulders to force me to sit on the beanbag. He stared into my eyes. "What's wrong?"

"I don't think she can breathe!" Lola placed her hand on my forehead, and then she pulled my hair away from my face. "Ruby, did you put peanuts in those cookies?"

"NO! I never cook with nuts." Ruby looked terrified.

"We need to take her home!" Hunter lifted me up on my feet and put his shoulder under one arm. "Kendall, grab her other side."

Kendall did. Then we shoved our way down the staircase, turning sideways to avoid the tree trunk that curves a little into the staircase. They dragged me over to the picnic bench a few feet away from the blind and sat me down.

"Put your head between your knees," Hunter said.

I did, staring down at my fingernails. They were greenish.

"Someone call Uncle Jake or Aunt Maggie," Kendall fidgeted with her bag on her hip. "My phone's dead."

"No!" I threw my hand up to stop the nonsense. No need to get the parents involved when it could earn me a quick, one-way ticket to Arizona.

"But you can't breathe." Lola knelt down next to me and lifted my head up to look into her eyes. "Allie, I'm worried about you. You keep having asthma attacks. What's going on?"

I took a couple of deep breaths, and to my surprise, they went in that time. I raised my head to look at my four cousins who had concern written all over their faces.

"I think I'm good now. I don't know what happened. Maybe it was anxiety or something." I stood up, stretched, and took another two deep breaths.

"You look a little better," Ruby said. "I'll go get your stuff so you don't have to climb back up the stairs."

Ruby ran back up to the blind, leaving an awkward silence behind. I needed to change the subject.

"Let's do the initiation this weekend," I said. "At dinner tonight, we can ask Mamaw if we can all come for a sleepover."

"Are you sure you're going to feel well enough by the weekend?" Hunter's creased forehead and narrowed eyes staring at me made me nervous.

"Of course. I'm fine." I stood and took a deep breath. "See? Good as new."

Ruby finally ran back from the blind with my jacket and my emergency medical kit.

"We're having the initiation this weekend," Hunter told her "I can't wait. I'll show you girls. I'm a Carroway boy—through and through." Then he turned to me. "Allie, are you sure you're okay? Should I walk you back to your house?"

"No. I'm good. Really."

Hunter sighed. "That's a relief." Then he gave me that winning smile. "I better go change. See you at dinner!"

And he sped off.

"I hope that gator doesn't recognize him as a Carroway boy," Lola said.

Kendall put both hands on her cheeks.

"Poor Hunter! We're sendin' him to his doom."

"Don't you think you're both being a little dramatic? You'll see. This Uncle Andy thing is a big, fat, fabricated story used to scare little kids on camping trips. That's all it is."

"I want to believe that," Ruby said. "But . . ."

"But what?"

She held up her hands. "Where *are* all Mamaw's tablecloths?"

CHAPTER 10

Unwanted Clutter

Time was ticking, and I needed to get back home to clear the table for the filming of our family dinner. When Mom added "clearing the dinner table" to my chore list last year, I never thought we'd be doing dinner more than once in a day. Since all our TV shows end with a meal, let's just say we film ourselves eating a *lot*.

This time, when I walked in the door, I almost ran into a nicely-dressed middle-aged businesswoman wearing a butter-colored skirt-suit with matching heels.

"Hello," she said, and she stuck her pen into the side of her thick blonde, perfectly-styled hair. She held out her hand to shake mine. "You must be Allie."

I shook her hand and grinned.

"Yes, ma'am. That's me."

"Your mom said it was okay for me to come in."

"That's fine," I said. "People come and go out of here all the time."

"My name is Ellen. I'm from Bayou's Best Realty."

My gut cramped.

"Realty? Like in selling houses?"

Ellen nodded. "Yes. Selling *and* buying. Sometimes it's houses, sometimes property. I absolutely *love* your house."

"Me too. Except for the creaky ceiling and the flooded-out floor."

"What?" Ellen crossed her arms, but then laughed and brushed my comments away with her hand. "All easy fixes. A house this age is bound to have a few flaws. But the layout is perfect for a big family to entertain. And all the upgrades are simply fabulous."

An energy jolt rose from my toes to my throat.

"Are we selling our house?"

Ellen put her hand over her mouth, and her eyes shifted away from me.

"Oh, you'll want to talk to your parents about that. They called me out to bring them some information and to have a look around. I left a folder for them on your table over there." She pointed over toward the cluttered table and then held out her hand to shake again.

"It's been a pleasure, Allie."

"Likewise, ma'am. Can I walk you to the door?"

"Not necessary. I can see myself out."

"Okay."

"But don't forget to tell your mom about the folder."

"I won't."

"And, by the way, I've been praying for you and your allergies. It must be horrible to be allergic to nuts. I practically live on them."

"It's not so bad," I lied, and then I thought, With all these millions of people always praying for me, I should be healed by Thanksgiving and be able to eat a whole pecan pie without a problem.

The door closed behind Ellen, and I darted to the table to look for the folder.

It sat right on top of a stack of Bibles and devotional books, which sat next to an open laptop, a bag of potato chips, a plate of cookies, and a half-full plastic tumbler of iced-tea. And that sat next to my Math book, a cheerleading bow, and my unzipped backpack with all my pens and paper spilling out. That sat next to some wadded-up napkins and a box of cereal that I grabbed breakfast out of that morning.

I moved my backpack to the living room sofa, closed up the cereal box and placed it back in the pantry, and then sat down to read the contents of the folder.

The first page showed a picture of a large, white two-story house, with a big ugly cactus in the front yard. The backyard looked like it was part of a golf course.

And the address said it was in . . . Arizona.

Spacious and modern, the Joshua model is designed specifically for the homeowner who lives in this popular tourist destination. The "house-within-a-house" gives everyone the privacy needed when guests arrive for a long golf weekend, while providing an oversized great room for parties, fund-raising events, and family holiday gatherings . . .

Bleah.

I lifted the page out of the folder and walked it to the shredder. Before I could stop myself, the Joshua model was history.

I returned to the folder to read the next page.

It had a picture of my house on it!

Louisiana charm, with celebrity neighbors. This upgraded beauty will have you feeling like it's the holidays all year long because there's room for everyone! Multi-level, with five spacious bedrooms, a den, library, and game room. And don't forget the pool out back. Plus, you can wave to the famous Carroway family on your way to work. This one won't last!

On the bottom of the page was a picture of Ellen with her phone number listed next to the logo of Bayou's Best Realty.

This couldn't be happening.

My hand shook as I flipped to the next page. It was a boring printout of numbers that I couldn't read through the blur of tears that filled my eyes and threatened to drop and drench all the stupid pieces of paper.

And then a thought hit me. I had been focusing all my attention on adding a new cousin, but the reality was, we were going to lose one.

Me.

With the help of the adrenaline still raging through my system, I sped through the living area, clearing everything. I shoved shoes under the sofa, threw clothes and backpacks into the closet, and stacked the books, papers, and the dreaded folder on the table in the laundry room. I dropped the plastic cups in the sink, then pulled the red-checkered tablecloth out of the linen closet and spread it out on the table. As I smoothed the bumps out, I thought of how many tablecloths we own.

At least twenty. Could be thirty. They practically spill out of the closet every time I open it.

And then I thought of "the gator."

And for just one second, I wondered out loud, "Why *does* Mamaw only use placemats?"

The door at the side of the house opened, and in walked Zeke with that positive grin he always has plastered on his face.

"Allie, you're a treasure, you know that? The place looks great!"

Zeke's aware of our clutter and how I'm the one who always takes care of it. He rubbed his belly. "Food's coming in soon. You ready for us to set up?"

I nodded. "What are we having?"

Zeke wiggled his dark eyebrows up and down.

"Chicken and biscuits. Mac and cheese."

I didn't react. Even comfort food didn't sound good right now with my stomach still in knots.

"Zeke? How long do you think, until we really start filming? Hannah said four, but you know how it goes around here better than she does."

Zeke—who has a master's degree in counseling in addition to his killer directing skills—walked in a few feet closer and gave me the squinty-eyes.

"You okay, Allie-oop?"

I can never fool Zeke, so I just shook my head.

Zeke pulled up a chair and sat down near me.

"Hmmm. Anything I can do?"

I shook my head again.

"It must be bad if you're not talking." Zeke ran both hands back through the top of his short, curly black hair and then clasped them both behind his neck.

I shrugged.

"It might be. I'm not sure. I need some time to figure it all out."

Zeke tilted his head to stretch his neck, first to the left, then to the right. He glanced at the gigantic round clock in our living room, and leaned his chair on the back two legs.

"We're not going to need you till five o'clock. You think that's enough time to find your smile?"

"Maybe."

"Okay then. Get outta here." He pointed at me. "And don't worry about the smile. If it doesn't come back with you, we'll just stuff a biscuit in your mouth and film that."

"Deal."

I turned to leave, and Zeke called after me. "Allie?'

I stopped but didn't turn around. "Yeah?"

"You know who you *can* talk to, right?"

I grabbed for the doorknob. "That's where I'm going right now."

"Good. I'll see you at five."

I opened the door and ran for the Diva.

CHAPTER 11

Heart to Heart

In minutes, I was lying face down in the turquoise beanbag.

I tried not to cry since I didn't want a puffy face for filming, but I couldn't help it.

God was going to take me away from Louisiana. And Mamaw and Papaw. And my cousins. All the places I loved. How could this be? Just because of stupid allergies?

I pounded the beanbag with my fist.

"I don't want to go, God! Can't you heal me? Wouldn't it be better for me to stay here with all of my family? I don't understand!"

I hit the beanbag three more times. And then I was out of breath again, so I stopped talking.

And that's when God started talking to me. Well, I didn't hear any out-loud voice, just a soft whisper in my heart.

Breathe, Allie. I am in charge of everything, even the air that goes into your lungs. Trust me.

I turned onto my side, took a shallow breath, and stared up at all the Scripture boards I had pounded into the "Allie wall." One of them caught my eye, so I got up to look at it more closely.

"Trust in the Lord with all your heart. Lean not on your own understanding. In all your ways acknowledge him and he will make your paths straight."

This was Ruby's favorite verse. She gave this plaque to me in the hospital the day I almost died after eating the peanut butter cookie. I wondered if I would ever be a "regular kid" after that day. The answer, since then, had been no.

Nothing about me is regular.

Is that good or bad, God?

I rested my forehead on the plaque, as if maybe the truth of the words in the verse would soak in and fill my useless understanding. Maybe I was panicking for no reason. There could be lots of reasons that both a home appraiser and a realtor would visit my house in one day, right?

Right. I was toast. Arizona burnt toast.

My breathing became more difficult, which made me mad. Being in the Diva was supposed to calm me down not make me more anxious. I pulled my phone out of my pocket and pulled up some music. I pressed play on one of my favorite hymns: "It Is Well with My Soul."

This version was actually the one that I, Kendall, Ruby, and Lola sang in church last year. People cried when we sang it, and I didn't really understand why. Probably because everything was going well with me at the time. It was a little different listening to it now.

When peace like a river attendeth my way, when sorrows like sea billows roll. Whatever my lot, thou has taught me to say, it is well, it is well, with my soul.

My "lot" was kind of stinking right now. Did God really want to teach me to say it's okay?

"I'm not a very good student, God," I said out loud. "But I'll try."

And I sang out loud with the recording through the rest

of the song. Somewhere in the middle of it, I tried to imagine Hunter's crackly voice singing the echo part, and it made me laugh. And that made me think of the initiation—set to take place this weekend.

Just maybe one of our last fun things together as cousins before I moved.

CHAPTER 12

Setting Up the Table

There we sat, throwing rolls at each other. The cousins, I mean. And we only really threw one roll, several times. And that was only after Kendall accidentally dropped it on the floor, and my dog, Hazel Mae, licked it.

Hunter nailed Lola in the shoulder.

"Hey, isn't it enough that you've already launched several frogs at me today?"

"Just working on my trajectory," Hunter said. Then he smiled big.

Lola smoothed her shiny short hair and tried to hide the pink streak under some other layers when the cameraman came her way.

Then she grabbed the roll and sent it flying my way.

"Hey! I didn't launch any frogs at you."

"I know, but you were the one who called us all up there for the secret meeting. We were sitting ducks."

"Shhh. If you keep talking loud, the other table will hear and start asking questions."

Kendall, who was sitting next to me and had been taking a couple of selfies wearing yet another new choker, leaned into the table and talked in a low voice.

"Maybe this is a good time to ask Mamaw about the

weekend, while we're filming and all. The parents will more likely go along with it."

"Oooh. Good idea," I said.

Usually, we have a rough script of things to say during filming. After we do that, they just let us freestyle, and more often than not someone says something original but hilarious that ends up in the final cut of the episode. That's what we were doing right then, when all the roll throwing was going on.

"Okay, here I go. Hunter," I pointed in his direction, "play along."

Hunter nodded.

I cleared my throat. "Mamaw Kat? Can I ask you something?"

The adults at the other table all turned their heads to look over at me.

Mamaw finished chewing and swallowing her biscuit. "What is it, sweet girl?"

"Umm . . . I was wondering, since we don't have school or filming on Friday, can all of us come and spend the afternoon and then sleep over with you at your house?"

"The whole family?" Mamaw's face lit up. She *loves* when we all come over.

"No, just me, Lola, Ruby, and Kendall."

"Why, that would be wonderful!" Mamaw said. "I know! We can sleep out on the porch, like old times."

"Not likely," Papaw Ray said. "Got a storm comin'. Could end up with a bunch of screamin' mimis in the house with us all night. Is that what you want, Kat?"

"Aw, Ray, they don't really scream anymore. Look at 'em. They're almost teenagers. And if it rains, we can pop popcorn and watch movies inside."

"That sounds like fun. Can I come?" Hunter found his cue perfectly.

"No!" Kendall said. "It's just us girls."

"Kendall . . ." Aunt Kassie did not look happy.

This was playing out just as I had hoped.

"Allie," Mom added, "why does it have to be just a girl thing?"

"I vote for Hunter," Papaw Ray said. "I don't want to be overrun by females. We can go fishin' if the storm goes the other way."

"Fishing sounds great!" Hunter said, and he turned in our direction and winked.

Lola continued the charade. "I guess we could let you come, Hunter. But can you take a bath or something first? Or change into clean socks? Boys your age smell really bad at the end of the day."

"*Lola!*" Lola's mom Janie threw a napkin ball in her direction.

Ruby giggled. "But it's true."

I thought that hearing us complain about smelly boys might bring our dads into the conversation, but they just kept eating and talking about using golf clubs to hit random things into the water.

"I say, no Hunter, no girls." Papaw Ray took a long drink of iced tea and then wiped his bearded chin with a napkin. "And if y'all get to squealin' in the night, I'm sendin' ya home."

"That seems reasonable," Mamaw said. "It's gonna be soooo fun, havin' my grandkids come and spend the night with me."

"So, is it okay with all the moms and dads?" I figured I'd just make sure while we were all sitting there together.

The dads were still talking, but the moms all agreed we could do it—as long as Hunter was included in the plans.

If only they knew that he *was* the plan.

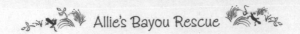

"Allie has a doctor's appointment on Friday at eleven," Mom said. "We'll swing back by here, have lunch, and then I'll drive y'all out—as long as the weather cooperates."

Papaw Ray shook his head. "Never known Louisiana weather to cooperate, but we'll see."

CHAPTER 13

Dark Clouds

Thursday morning started out bright and sunny, but by mid-afternoon, threatening clouds had moved in. And while we all waited for the raindrops to materialize outside, a class four hurricane was brewing inside.

"Allie," Mom ruffled through some papers on the coffee table in the living room. "When you were cleaning up last night, did you happen to see a manila folder anywhere?"

"Ummm . . ."

"Ummm, what? Either you saw it or you didn't."

Mom came over to stand by me at the kitchen counter. I turned, stepped toward the sink, and began to rinse some dishes and put them in the dishwasher.

"What are you doing?"

"Clearing the sink. Helping you with the dishes."

Mom placed her hand on my forearm. "Stop, Allie."

"Why?" I stopped, pulled away from Mom, and crossed my arms.

"My dear, sweet daughter, you are helpful in many ways, but washing dishes is not usually one of them. What's up?"

Mom motioned for me to sit down on the dreaded barstool, but I stayed right where I was and began rinsing out a cup.

Mom sighed. "Allie, where's the folder? Your dad's coming home for just a few minutes, and I need to show it to him."

I finished rinsing the cup and then clunked it into the dish drainer. Thankfully, we use a lot of plastic around my house.

"It's in the laundry room."

Mom threw up her hands and headed to the laundry room. In seconds, she returned, pulled up a barstool, placing that horrible "folder of doom" in front of her.

"I shredded the first page," I said quietly, as she opened it.

Mom looked up. "You what?"

Here's when the wind really picked up.

"I shredded it. I'm sorry."

Mom's mouth dropped open, but she said nothing. She rifled through the folder, and then got up to pull the shredded ball of paper strips that used to be the "Joshua plan" out of the trash.

She threw the ball on the counter. "Tape it back together, please."

"What?"

"I said, tape it back together. You had no right to destroy my personal papers."

"I think I have every right when your personal papers have to do with me moving to Arizona. Why does everyone else know everything about me but me?"

Mom pulled a roll of tape from the junk drawer and flicked it over to me.

"Start taping."

I grabbed the tape dispenser and the strips of the shredded paper.

"Are you serious?"

"As a heart attack," she said.

"Or a mold allergy?" I pulled out a piece of tape and tried

to connect some of the strips, but it was impossible to make them match up.

Mom didn't say a thing. She just sat there and read the contents of the folder while I taped. It took me a while, but I got the job done.

I handed the unreadable paper back to Mom.

"Here. I'm sorry I ruined it."

She reached over and patted my hand. "Thank you."

"For the record, I don't like cactus."

"I don't like it either."

"Then why are we moving to a cactus town?"

"Who says we're moving?"

"Everyone! I told you, everyone knows everything about me but me!"

Dad walked in the door just then and looked like he had seen a beaver in the middle of the kitchen table or something.

"What's goin' on in here? Why all the yellin'?"

"Allie thinks we're moving to Arizona without telling her," Mom said.

Dad came over and put his arm around me.

"Now, you know we would never move and leave you here all alone without some kind of warnin'."

I pushed him away. "Not funny. You know what Mom means."

"Yeah, I do, but I'm not real sure why you're all worked up. If we were plannin' on moving we would let you know before we told anyone else."

"That's what upsets me. You would just 'let me know,' not ask me what I think about it."

"Allie, you're twelve, you shouldn't be worryin' about this stuff."

"Dad! Twelve-year-olds worry! A *lot*!"

"Well, you should stop worryin' and trust your parents to do the right thing for you."

"It's not that easy. Especially when you're talking about moving to Arizona."

"We haven't even talked about *that* yet." Dad put both hands on my shoulders and looked me in the eyes.

"But I do want you to understand *this*. I'm your father, and I love you more than anything in this world. So, if a doctor tells me tomorrow that we have to move to Timbuktu in order to save you, then you can bet that we'll be movin' to Timbuktu—lickety split!"

"And I would have no say?"

Dad sighed, took his hands off my shoulders, and went over to sit next to Mom.

"If I gave you a say, what *would* you say?"

I looked at him and thought a moment.

He waved his index finger in the air.

"And before you answer that, think a minute. If staying here in Louisiana would make you sicker, but moving somewhere else would make you well, *then* what would you say? What if *you* were the parent? What if we were talkin' about one of your brothers or one of your cousins? Would you choose to stay here and watch them get sicker and sicker?"

I looked down at the floor. A sob threatened to emerge from my throat. I wiped a tear from one eye before it could drip and ruin my argument.

"Allie." Mom's voice was gentle and soft. "We're just doing some preliminary research. We have a creative God, and we know he's up to something with this situation. There are all

kinds of options. Many of them don't even involve cactus, or Arizona."

I looked back up and spied a tissue box. I had to get to it before more tears spilled from my eyes. My nose was threatening to leak too.

"Can I go outside for a while?"

Dad glanced out the window. "Take an umbrella. Those clouds look ready to let loose any minute."

"Don't go far," Mom said. "We're having an early dinner since your dad is filming tonight."

"I'm just going to the Diva," I told them.

"That's fine," Dad said. "Just give what we talked about some thought. You're my princess, you know, and I'll do anything to rescue you when you're in distress."

"Bleah. I hate being called princess."

"That's fine. But you are a daughter of the King." Dad pointed up to the ceiling. "And he loves you more than I do. So think about that."

I ran to the coat closet and put on my hooded raincoat and some rain boots.

Then I ran out the door, wiping my escaping tears on my arm.

The rain was just starting to fall when I reached the Diva. I squeaked open the gate and flew up the stairs. I didn't raise the awnings since I didn't want the wind blowing all that wet stuff in. The awnings were a fairly new feature at the Diva—Dad had added them last year when we told him what a pain it was to try to dry everything out after every rain.

I wondered for a second how much rain they get in Arizona.

I fumbled around to turn on the two battery-powered lanterns we have sitting on tables for dark times such as this. The glow from each light cast my shadow on the walls as I walked around reading Bible verses.

Weeping may last for the night, but joy comes in the morning. Psalm 30:5

I wrote that one up there when my favorite dog, Pokey, got hit by a car and died last year. He should have been faster, running across that street! I cried so hard that night, and I never thought I'd feel joy again. And then Dad brought that licking-machine Hazel Mae home. And ever since then, she has licked me on the cheek to wake me up in the morning, and I laugh.

The thunder rolled outside and the now heavy rain plunked on the roof and against the awnings.

"Hey, who's up there! Don't you know it's gonna flood soon?"

A familiar voice rang up through the rumbles and pitter-patters.

Hunter.

Since the awnings weren't open, I couldn't just lean over and look down, so I made my way down the stairs.

There he stood at the gate.

"Gator Buster," he said, and then he grinned that funny grin. He wasn't wearing a raincoat, and his short blond hair was wet and curling up on top of his head. His glasses were fogged a little, and his clothes were drenched.

"What are you doing here?" My mind was still a little mushy from holding back the tears. I stared down at his bare calves. "And why are you wearing those basketball shorts in this freezing weather?"

"I always wear shorts if I have a choice. So, is the temporary password still good? Or is that just a one-time use thing?"

It dawned on me that he wanted me to let him into the Diva.

"Oh. Well, I don't think we've ever had someone come for a return visit. Let me think." I tapped my cheek with my index finger.

"Think fast," Hunter said. "It's gonna pour in a minute."

Water sprinkled down upon us through the tree branches. A big drop landed on Hunter's forehead and ran down his nose. He opened his mouth and caught the moisture on his tongue, which made me laugh.

"Come on up, Gator Buster," I said, and we made it up right as the clouds let loose.

"Whoa, good thing I brought snacks," Hunter said. "We could be here a while."

He took the top off the white bucket he was carrying and pulled out a tube of barbequed potato chips, a sleeve of mini-powdered donuts, a bag of chocolate chips, and a bottle of green Gatorade.

"Wow. You don't mess around when it comes to junk food."

Hunter ripped open the chocolate chips and poured some into my hand.

"Yeah, good thing you aren't allergic to chocolate."

"Yes. I'm very grateful for that."

I poured a few of the cold, hard chocolate pieces into my mouth and chomped.

"I wish we had some *hot* chocolate right now."

"And marshmallows," Hunter added.

"What else you got in that bucket?" I hoped Hunter would say a hot bowl of mac and cheese. I needed a little comfort food at the moment.

"Just duct tape," Hunter said. "It always comes in handy."

The wind pounded the awnings, and I got up and pulled a couple of fleece blankets out of a light purple cabinet that Mamaw Kat had bought at a garage sale.

"Here," I handed one to Hunter. "Dry yourself off with this. You can sit over there in that saucer chair. I know it's pink, but it's super comfortable."

I plunked down in my usual turquoise-glitter beans.

Hunter peeked over at the chair and hesitated.

"I prefer to stand." He opened up the folded blanket and wrapped it around his shoulders, then began mulching on the chips. Not munching. *Mulching*. The sound was deafening.

"Allie," Hunter took a break from the chips to take a swig of the Gatorade and swallowed. "I hesitate to divulge this kind of information to you—the chairman of the Duck Diva initiation committee—but since you're going to be my cousin and all—"

"What is it? Is something wrong?" I didn't think my stomach could take anymore bad news today.

"I guess I should just confess."

I sat up straighter.

"Confess? What? You didn't share your password with anybody, did you?"

"Password? No! I would never betray the committee."

"Then what?"

Hunter paced a little and mulched some more. I just watched and hoped he would land soon. He did, finally in the pink chair.

"I'm gonna fail the initiation. I just know it. I'm not cut out to be a Carroway. I'm not like any of you. It's written all over my face. 'Not. A. Carroway.' See?"

Hunter swiped the back of his hand across his face. He positioned his fingers in the shape of an L for "Loser."

He went on.

"I'm sure Kassie and Wayne are thinking the same thing. I wouldn't be surprised if they change their mind about the adoption and next week instead of becoming your cousin, I'll be back in the foster system hoping some other family will take me in."

"That's crazy talk." I walked over and looked in his bucket. "How much junk have you consumed today? I think you're on a sugar low."

"This is my first snack of the day. And it's happened before," Hunter said.

"What are you talking about?"

"This is my third time being 'considered' for adoption."

"Well, those people were nuts to send you back. They didn't deserve you."

"Oh yeah? How do you know? Maybe a loser is what they really did deserve."

"Hunter! I think your mood is being affected by the weather. It happens to me a lot. The truth gets crowded out by the clouds."

"Truth?"

"Yeah. The truth is, you've already been chosen by all of us to be in our family. So that means you are. Case closed. Nobody's gonna change their mind. Even if you fling a thousand frogs in my hair."

"But I could fail the initiation."

I thought about the four events we had planned for this poor boy. Mud and frogs, singing, hunting and cooking, and hanging out in a haunted storage shed. I figured he might be able to get two out of the four.

I suddenly felt bad for making this agreement with the girls. Kendall for sure wouldn't give up the Diva if Hunter didn't pass.

I grabbed a donut out of Hunter's bucket and chewed on that a minute. The wind continued to beat on the awnings, and the rain came down heavy now. A stream of water began dripping from a leak in the roof—right on top of my beanbag.

Hunter noticed the drip, emptied his bucket, and placed it under the leak.

"Thanks," I said.

"You're welcome. You know, this is a really old structure."

"Yeah, it's ancient! Our dads used to play in here when they were kids."

Hunter sniffed. "It also smells weird. Have you ever noticed that?"

I laughed. "That's just Kendall's perfume."

"Possible." He looked around some more, pushed on a couple of support beams, and surveyed the ceiling. "I think we can do better with this place. In fact, I've been working on some architectural drawings that could add square footage without putting anymore stress on the tree . . ."

"You want to add on?"

"Yeah, why not? You never know, Kassie and Wayne might decide to adopt another foster child. Or your parents might."

"I doubt that. They seem to have their hands full with me and all my problems."

"Either way, we should plan for the future."

"Hunter, I might be moving."

I couldn't believe I blurted that out. It came just as some

thunder roared, so I hoped maybe he hadn't heard it. But then, when I saw his eyes widen, sending a shocked look my way, I knew he had.

"Moving? You mean to a different house in the neighborhood?"

"No. Somewhere drier. Like Arizona. Or Timbuktu."

"Timbuktu? Is that a real place?"

"I don't . . . uh . . . I never . . . I don't know."

"But what about the TV show?"

Carried Away with the Carroways was my only hope at this point. Maybe somewhere in the contract it said we had to live in Louisiana or get sued.

"We might just have to be the Arizona Carroways who come back home to visit from time to time."

"That's not good." Hunter slammed his chip tube on the teacart. I worried as I watched Kendall's giraffe wobble.

"No, it's not."

Hunter turned, and slouched.

"This is a horrible, gloomy day."

"I know."

"And I'm going to fail the initiation."

"Maybe. But it could be fun, right?"

"Sure! Just like you moving to Timbuktu could be fun."

Just as Hunter said that, lightning must have hit the ground right next to us. The place lit up like Christmas, and the rumble practically knocked us to the ground.

"Allie!" Dad's voice, followed by his shrill whistle, cut through the pounding rain. "Time to get back in the house!"

"I gotta go, and you better too," I said. "I'll see you tomorrow."

Hunter wrapped the junk food and duct tape in the blanket and left the bucket to catch the rain.

"Okay, tomorrow. Any insider tips for me? Is that fair to ask?"

"No, it's not. But I'll give you one, because you shared your snacks, and because I really do want you to succeed."

"Okay." Hunter's face froze looking at me.

"Practice singing," I said.

"Singing?"

"Yeah. Singing."

Thunder cracked again.

"*Allie!*" Dad's voice was closer now.

"Coming!" I shut off the lanterns, and Hunter and I scrambled down the steps of the Diva. Water rushed down the branches and spilled all over us on the way down.

"I hope the river doesn't rise too high tonight," Hunter said.

"You never know," I said. "This place gets a lot of water. We'll just have to wait and see what happens."

"Yep, we'll see."

Hunter flew up and over the hill toward his house, gone in a flash.

"Allie, come on, girl!" Dad had reached me and grabbed me by the arm. "Even the bullfrogs are taking cover. Let's get in the warm house."

We both started a jog toward the house, but it felt like a sprint to me. I was out of breath in seconds. When I got in the house, I didn't even have the energy to take my coat or boots off. Mom had to peel them off, and while she did, Dad grabbed a blanket, wrapped me up in it, and carried me to the sofa by the fireplace.

"What's going on, Allie-girl?" Dad looked scared as he stroked my cheek.

I couldn't talk. All I could do was concentrate on grabbing my next breath. And every time I tried to exhale, I felt like something was clamping around my chest, producing that high-pitched whistle that was becoming a daily companion.

Dad stood up and walked over to Mom, who was on the phone with someone.

"We've gotta get a handle on this, Maggie," he said.

"We will, Jake. We will."

CHAPTER 14

Doctor Shocker

Allie, I want you to take a deep breath and then blow into this device until all the air is out of your lungs."

I took the air-flow device from Dr. Snow, said a quick prayer, breathed in, and then blew out with all my might. That high-pitch whistle made an appearance again.

"Nice wheeze," Dr. Snow said, and he took back the device and held it up to his face to read the numbers on the side.

"You're not getting a lot of air these days, are you, Allie?"

"I've been okay most of the time." I tried not to show any signs of being out of breath, even though I was.

"I beg to differ. This machine tells all. Your numbers are really low and . . ."

He reached over and pulled the skin down under my right eye with his thumb, just like my mom does all the time.

"You've got some nice dark circles under your eyes, which is unusual for a kid."

"Thanks. I was looking for an excuse to get to use some makeup."

"You don't need makeup, you need your airways to open up. Something is causing them to shut down."

"Is it mold?" Mom sat on the edge of her chair over in the corner.

Dr. Snow flipped through the pages of my file and shook his head a few times.

"Could be," he said. "It's the only new thing that cropped up on the latest allergy tests. It's been extra wet around here lately, and after the latest flood, I have been seeing a lot more of my mold sufferers here in the office."

Dr. Snow reached for the computer keyboard and began typing.

"I'm going to start you with an inhaler." He handed me back the air-flow device.

"Use this three times a day to start. If the numbers register below this red line, take two puffs on the inhaler. And of course, when you have an attack, take two puffs. I'm thinking that you've been dealing with this for a while, and you might not even realize that you are low on air."

"She looks tired all the time."

"Thanks, Mom."

"That sounds right to me." Dr. Snow finished typing and then spun his chair around to face Mom. "It's very tiring when you can't get air. From what I can tell, Allie's gotten to the point of having out-of-control asthma. Imagine a glass filled with water right to the top. Every drop sends water spilling over the edge. That's her bronchial tubes right now. Any little allergen is closing them down. She needs to give her body a break for a while, so she can get to a place where she isn't so sensitive and things can calm down."

Dr. Snow began typing again, and spoke while he clicked with a mouse.

"I'm going to print out some instructions for mold-proofing your house. It's a daunting task to get to it all at once, especially if your house is over twenty years old. You already live in a damp climate which is working against you."

Mom glanced over at me, and I could read her thoughts.

Arizona would be better.

Dr. Snow stopped typing and walked over to the printer, where he pulled out about ten sheets of information. He handed the stack to my mom.

"Start with Allie's room and the rooms where she spends most of her time.

"Don't let Allie clean out anything at this point. If there are any mold spores anywhere in there, we don't want her inhaling them."

Mom began to read the printout. "Remove all stuffed animals and decorative pillows?"

Dr. Snow nodded. "They're the absolute worst."

"You are taking away my happiness right now," I said.

"Remove carpet if possible?" Mom scratched her head. "This is going to be quite a project. Our house was built in the 70s." She continued to read through the printout.

Dr. Snow sat back down on his chair.

"Try not to be overwhelmed. Just do what you can, and we'll check back with you in two weeks and see how things are going."

I was relieved that he wasn't writing a prescription for Timbuktu . . . yet.

"But . . ."

Uh oh. Here it comes.

"Bring her right in if she has any more serious episodes."

He turned to me. "You can add the breath measurer and

the inhaler to your Allie-Kit." Then he winked and reached over to pat me on the side of the shoulder.

Great. At the rate I was going I was going to have to start carrying a full-sized backpack just for all my medical needs.

"Do you ladies have any questions for me?"

My questions at this point were not for Dr. Snow. They were for God. Well, I only had one question really.

WHY *is this happening right now*?

"I have one, Dr. Snow," Mom said. "Allie and her cousins have a sleepover planned at their grandparents' house tonight. As you know, it's right next to the river, and with the weather the way it is, I was wondering if we should reschedule."

Oh, whoops. *This* couldn't be happening. My mind went into overdrive trying to figure out what to do if Dr. Snow told us I couldn't go tonight.

"Hmmm." Dr. Snow stroked his chin and looked into my supposedly glassy eyes with the dark circles. "It gets pretty swampy out there, Allie."

"It's really important that I go," I said.

"It's more important for you to breathe," Mom said.

Dr. Snow must have seen desperation in my eyes, because he winked again.

"I'll be right back," he said, and he jetted out of the room.

"Mom . . ."

She cut me off before I could plead.

"Allie, this is not up for debate. Whatever Dr. Snow says goes. Case closed."

"Yes, ma'am." I slumped my shoulders and prepared to call the whole initiation thing off and pack my bags for Arizona.

Dr. Snow charged through the door right then, which

caused me to almost slide off the slippery-papered exam table. He had a box in his hand, which he opened to reveal an inhaler.

"Here you go. I had one sample left. I'd like you to take a couple of puffs right now and see what happens."

Dr. Snow instructed me to do just the opposite of what I had done with the air-flow measuring device. This time I was supposed to breathe out all the way, then inhale the contents of the inhaler, hold my breath a second, then relax my breath out.

I did it twice. The propellant felt cold and weird going down my throat.

Mom and Dr. Snow stared at me like I was going to turn colors or something.

Instead, I just got a little shaky.

"Are you okay, honey? How do your lungs feel?"

"It could take her a few minutes to notice anything. But, take a look at her face, Maggie."

Mom looked at me and put her hands up to her cheeks. "What?"

"You've got some color goin' on, sister."

"What color? Green? Purple?" I snuck a look down at my fingertips. They looked okay.

"It's more like rose," Dr. Snow said. "How you should look."

"Does that mean it's working?" I prayed and prayed without saying a single word out loud. God knew what I was asking for.

"I'd say for now, you're going to be okay. Take two puffs on the inhaler tonight before bed, and stay out of the rain, and you should be okay at your grandparents' house."

I wanted to jump off the exam table and hug Dr. Snow. But that would have looked suspicious. So, I just stayed still—well, except for my hands that were still jittering.

"Thank you," I said.

"You're welcome. You know that you're my favorite celebrity patient, so I don't want to take away ALL your happiness in one visit."

"Ha! I'm probably your only celebrity patient."

He laughed. "Yep. Pretty much. None of the other Carroway kids seem to get sick much."

I was highly aware of that.

"Well, have fun at the sleepover, and call or email me if you have any questions."

"You got it."

"Great."

"Thanks, Dr. Snow," Mom said.

"My pleasure." And with that, my favorite and best doctor in the whole-wide-world departed into the hallway, and I hoped I wouldn't be seeing him again for a long time.

CHAPTER 15

The Trouble Begins

The windshield wipers on our SUV could barely keep up with the rain on the way home from the doctor's appointment.

"Allie, can you call Mamaw and ask her what it's like out at their place?"

Mom squinted to see out of the window, and slowed the car down a little.

Mamaw answered in a flash.

"Please don't be callin' me sayin' you're not comin'. I've been making food all day, and I have snickerdoodles in the oven."

I smiled. Snickerdoodles, yum.

"Mamaw, is it raining out at your place? It's pouring here."

I put her on speaker so Mom could hear.

"Oh, what's a little rain? It's not gonna hurt anything."

That didn't sound good.

"Kat, is the river rising? I'm worried it's gonna flood out there."

"It's coming up a little bit. But Papaw says the storm is going the other direction. He's been watching it all day, he hasn't gone to get sandbags, and he hasn't moved any machinery yet. That's a good sign. You know how he is about that."

"Well . . . it's pretty bad up here right now."

Mom drove through a deep puddle and then had to pump the breaks to stop at the red light.

"I'm gonna see what Jake says and I'll let you know."

"You tell him that his mama wants to eat cookies with her grandkids."

"Yeah, Mom," I said. "Don't forget to tell Dad about the cookies."

"See you soon, Allie-gal," Mamaw said. "I got some new board games for us play too."

I just love my Mamaw Kat. She always has fun stuff for us to do when we go to her house. Only this time, we needed her to not be so fun so we could conduct Hunter's initiation.

Mom pushed the remote for the garage door, and as it opened, it revealed Kendall, Hunter, Lola, and Ruby standing there with overnight bags at their feet. Mom pulled in halfway, leaving the back of the car exposed to the rain.

"Mom dropped us off so you wouldn't have to waste time coming to pick us up." Kendall adjusted her eggplant-colored choker and hummed a little tune.

Dad popped his head out of the door that lead from the house to the garage.

"Oh, good, you're back." He smirked. "These kids showed up and are driving me nuts. You need to take them a long way away from here."

Dad came all the way out and pushed Hunter halfway across the garage until they began to wrestle a little. Then he put him in a headlock.

"You can leave Hunter if you want, but take all these giggly girls to Mamaw's."

Hunter grinned as he fought to escape. "Papaw Ray needs me to fish with him, remember?"

Dad let Hunter go and brushed off his shirt. "Oh, yeah.

Then I better not damage you. He's gonna need someone to clean up all the fish guts."

Dad picked up the bags and began throwing them in the back of the SUV from the second seat since the tailgate was hanging out in the rain.

"Jake," Mom said. "Do you think it's safe to take the kids out there? It's raining pretty hard."

"It's safer than dealing with Mamaw if we don't." Dad walked over and gave Mom a kiss on the forehead. "I'll drive 'em so you can go wrap up in a blanket by the fire."

Mom sighed. "Bless you."

"Okay, kids, get in the car! If we don't get a move on, we're gonna have to paddle out to Mamaw's."

"I need to get my stuff," I yelled, and I ran into the house for my suitcase.

Mom pulled me close and kissed me on the cheek. "Remember to stay inside, and don't let that inhaler out of your sight. If you have any problems, tell Mamaw and then call me right away."

"Yes, ma'am. Thanks for letting me go tonight."

"You're welcome, sweetie." Mom hugged me again. "I love you more than anything."

"I know. I love you, too." I grabbed my suitcase from her and met everyone else back in the garage.

"Hang on," Ruby said. "I need to put our snack cooler in." She walked over to a far corner of the garage and grabbed a beat-up, blue ice chest.

"I'm sitting by you," I said. "I'm starving."

Ruby giggled. "I call the way-back seat." Then she turned to me and winked.

"Hunter, do you want to sit up front with my dad?" I didn't know what Ruby had in that cooler, but if she was winking, I figured it must be good.

"Yeah, Hunter," Dad said. "Guys up front."

Hunter jumped in the front seat and buckled up. Lola and Kendall took the second seat, leaving me and Ruby in the way, way back.

"Hope y'all brought your life jackets!" Dad said. Then he started up the SUV and pulled out of the garage.

Before we even got out of our driveway, I pulled the cooler onto my lap.

Ruby's eyes grew wide, and she shook her head.

"Aw, come on. I want to see what you brought."

Ruby put her hand on the lid and held it tight.

"It's a surprise," she whispered. "One that you don't want yet. Trust me."

"O . . . kay." I wedged the cooler back down on the floor between us. A hunger pang reminded me that I hadn't eaten lunch. "Dad, can we run through a drive-thru and get some burgers?"

Dad glanced at me in the rearview mirror. "Now that's a good idea!" And instead of stopping at any of the regular fast-food choices, Dad stopped right at the edge of town at the Bomb Burger Barbeque—home of the famous Kablooey Burger. A burger that is so messy you practically have to eat it with a spoon to keep it from exploding into your lap.

"Okay," Dad said, "Everybody out. We'll get our food to go. If Mr. Dimple is in there, try not to get into a conversation with him."

"That's next to impossible," Lola said.

"Just don't make eye contact." Kendall put both hands up next to her face. "Look straight ahead. No turning left or right."

"Focus," Ruby said.

"But he's so nice," Lola said. "And I like hearing about his latest inventions."

"He's an inventor?" Hunter asked. "That sounds interesting!"

"It is," Dad said. "But we don't have two hours to sit and listen to every detail today."

He swung the door open.

"Well, hello, Carroway family! How are you all on this wet fall day?"

Mr. Dimple sat in the right corner booth, munching on something messy.

"Hello, Rex. How are you doin'?" Dad walked over and shook Mr. Dimple's hand and then kept moving toward the ordering counter. We all followed along, as did Mr. Dimple.

"Why, I'm doin' just fine. Tryin' to figure out a way to keep my chickens dry."

"You could build them a house," Hunter said.

Oh. No. Hunter. You did not just say that.

Mr. Dimple grinned and put his hand on his chin.

"Well, it's quite a coincidence you should say that, young man. Let me show you what I'm designin' right now . . ."

Mr. Dimple took out a notepad from a big pocket in his one-piece, green work suit, and started flipping through the pages.

"We'll have six Kablooey combos with iced teas to go," Dad said to Wanda at the counter. Wanda raised her eyebrows. "Are you eating them in Maggie's car?"

Dad nodded. "Better gimme lots of napkins."

"You got it, Jake." Wanda grabbed about fifty napkins and

shoved them in a bag of their own. "Where you headed with this crazy bunch in a storm?"

"Just out to my folks' house. Dropping them off for a sleepover with my mom."

"Sounds like a fun time. But aren't you worried about a flood? This rains comin' down pretty hard."

"Nah. Ray's got it monitored. He says it's headed east."

"Let's hope. I'm still drying out my furniture from the last flood."

Louisiana was having a tough year. The massive storm just a few weeks earlier had caused a flood that destroyed businesses and displaced many families from their homes.

"Burgers are up!" Wanda shoved several foam boxes in a large bag, and stuffed drinks in two carriers. "Be careful out there."

Dad grabbed the bag, and Lola and I took the drinks.

"Okay, gang. We're outta here."

The rain had let up just a bit, so we swung open the door and jogged to the car. Ruby opened the back door so I could hop up with the drinks and slide into my seat.

I had to step over the mysterious ice chest that was somehow calling to me to open it.

"Where's Hunter?" Dad looked around the parking lot. "Is he still in there talking to Dimple?"

Kendall shrugged. Dad sighed and got back out of the car.

As I sat down in the back seat, I lost my battle with curiosity, and I opened the cooler.

"Noooooo!" Ruby yelled.

Something big and green leaped out of the cooler and onto my hand holding the drink carrier.

"*Bullfrogs!*" Kendall squealed, as two more jumped out and pounced around on the car seats and backs.

"Catch them!" Lola flopped down on the floor of the SUV and tried to trap one of them. "You guys need to help me!"

One of the frogs jumped from the back seat to the middle seat, knocking over the bag with the Kablooey burgers.

"Got one!" Ruby held the big thing up.

"Allie, open the cooler, but not too much. I don't want the others to get out!"

I did, and Ruby squished him in.

"I got one!" Lola rolled around on her back on the floor, holding a chubby frog up above her head. She somehow managed to do a sit-up and crawl over to the cooler to put him in with his slimy friends.

"Where's the third one?" Kendall leaned over to look in the front seat. "Uncle Jake and Hunter are coming!" She picked up the burger bag, straightened the boxes inside, and set it on Hunter's seat.

"Here, froggy, froggy!" Lola scoured the floor like a vacuum, looking under seats, and poking her nose into every corner of the SUV.

"Get back in your seat. They're coming back." Kendall grabbed Lola by the sleeve and pulled her back up next to her just as Hunter and Dad got to the car. Lola's hair covered her whole face. She looked like a mop with a pink streak. "Everybody just act normal."

We all tried to keep straight faces. But act normal? How do you act normal when a bullfrog is loose in your car?

CHAPTER 16

Rocky Road

Hunter jumped in the car first.

"That Mr. Dimple is an interesting guy! And he's an architect. Maybe he can help us redesign the . . ."

Kendall put her hand over Hunter's mouth. "Why don't you just be quiet and hand us back our burgers, Hunter?"

My dad opened the driver's side door, and Hunter's eyes shifted over toward him. "Oh, yeah. Oops." He reached in the bag and pulled out a box with secret sauce leaking all over it. "Yuck! Kendall, this looks like yours."

Kendall reached in the napkin bag and carefully spread several out on her lap.

"I'm ready," she said. Hunter handed her the burger box and turned around to get some more out of the bag.

"I'll eat mine when we get to Mamaw's," Dad said. "I need to focus on driving the curves."

He started up the SUV and backed out of the parking space. As he pulled out of the parking lot and onto the highway, the third bullfrog crawled out onto the middle of the floor and stopped.

When I saw that, I lost it. The iced tea I had just sipped blew out my nose. Same thing happened to Ruby, and we both started laughing uncontrollably in the way-back seat.

"I need another napkin!" Ruby yelled, and Kendall flew one back to her.

"You girls need to keep it down back there," Dad said.

And then the bullfrog—who was still sitting there staring at us—croaked.

Thankfully, Lola had the presence of mind to burp at that same moment.

Dad glared at her through the rearview mirror, but then chuckled. "Lola? Was that you? You burp like your dad."

"Thanks, Uncle Jake."

At this point, we were all doubled over, laughing that kind of laugh where no sound comes out, you can't breathe, and your stomach muscles feel like they're going to cramp.

Hunter shook his head and took a bite of his burger. "Crazy girls."

The frog—still staring—crawled toward me and Ruby. It was almost like he was daring us to pounce.

Ruby reached for the lid of the cooler and gestured to me to go get him. I moved my Kablooey burger off my lap and stretched my arms out till they felt like they were coming unhinged from my shoulders.

The frog inched toward me

"Come on, big guy," I whispered.

"Hang on!" Dad yelled, and he slammed on the brakes! The back of the SUV skidded right, then left. The frog leaped forward, right into my lap. It croaked and Lola covered it up with another loud burp. I screamed a little, but then regained my composure and stuffed froggy into the cooler. I was able to wedge the ice chest down between Ruby's and my feet just as the SUV straightened out. Dad stopped the car at a pullout a few yards down the road.

"That was gnarly!" Hunter yelled.

Dad got out of the car, opened our back door, and looked in.

"Everybody all right back here? That car pulled onto the highway right in front of me! I'm sorry if I shook y'all up."

"It's okay, Dad. We're good." I had to stifle a chuckle, thinking about all those frogs that were stuck in the cooler at my feet.

"Maybe we should just turn around and go back home," Dad said.

"No! This is all too fun!" Hunter pleaded.

That caused me to laugh again. Hunter had no idea just how much fun we were having in the way-back seat.

Mamaw was so glad to see us she practically burst a vein in her neck. She hugged my dad like five times.

"Thank you so much for bringing my darlin' babies out to see me. We're gonna have so much fun!" Then she pushed my dad away. "You can go now."

"I will, just as soon as I explain to you about Allie's inhaler."

"Inhaler? What's goin' on with our sweet girl now?"

I rolled my eyes and then rolled my suitcase into the front kids' room. We have lots of kids' rooms at Mamaw's. The front room has two double beds where I normally sleep if I'm not sleeping out on the porch. That would be on rainy nights like this.

Kendall, Ruby, and Lola followed me. Hunter ran off somewhere, I assumed to find Papaw Ray.

Ruby carried the frog cooler into the room with us.

"Ruby, why did you bring bullfrogs? That was almost a disaster!"

Ruby shrugged and looked a little sad. "Hunting frogs is

easy for me, and I didn't want Hunter to fail my part of the initiation, so I went out this morning and got these guys. I figured we could throw them in that old mud hole out by the barn and let him chase them around. It will still be yucky, but at least he'll have a chance to catch some."

"Well, you could have at least warned me they were in there."

"I tried to. But you . . . were . . . too . . . hungry." Ruby grabbed her stomach and bent over laughing again. "Oh, boy, you should have seen your face when that bullfrog jumped on the drinks. Hilarious!"

"Hilarious for me was seeing Lola down on the floor. You're a pretty stylish bullfrog hunter, Pink Streak."

Lola smoothed her hair. "I bet I look ridiculous. Where's a mirror?" She took off toward a bathroom.

Kendall put her hand on my shoulder. "Allie, are you sure you still want to do the shed thing?" She walked over to a window and looked out at the gray stormy day.

"The shed thing? Are you still thinking that silly story is true?"

"Well, who is this Andy person then? I told you I've seen pictures."

"Then you'll have to show me." I pointed to all the bookshelves in this one room alone. "If the story is true, we should be able to find some evidence here."

"Girls!" Mamaw called from the kitchen. "The cookies are ready. I got some beads too, so we can all make matching bracelets!"

Lola emerged from the bathroom looking lovely again. "I hope the frogs were the last surprise of the evening."

If only.

CHAPTER 17

Pumping for Information

We girls barely got ourselves settled in at the counter when Papaw Ray and Hunter burst through the kitchen door, soaking wet.

"No fishin' today, friends," Papaw Ray said. "Could be a little flood comin' our way after all."

"Are you serious?" Mamaw smiled. "You mean I might be stuck here with all these grandkids?" She bit off a chunk of snickerdoodle, chewed, and swallowed. "What a blessing."

"I'm gonna help Papaw move some of the machines." Hunter's grin was ear-to-ear, and he was shaking. I wasn't sure if it was because he was excited or cold.

"After we're done out there, we're gonna go for some sandbags."

"Oh no, you don't," Mamaw said. "Hunter didn't come here to just work. Let him come back in with us after he helps move the machines."

Papaw Ray glanced at all the string and beads that were scattered on the counter.

"Looks like just a bunch of girly fun to me."

"We have some other stuff planned," Kendall said. "And we need Hunter."

Hunter looked over at us through his wet, fogging glasses and tried to wink.

Papaw Ray grabbed a warm Snickerdoodle off the cooling rack and took a bite. Then he scanned each of our faces.

"I think you're all up to somethin'."

Mamaw pushed him in the shoulder. "Kids are always up to somethin,' so you best be on your way and leave them up to it."

Papaw put his arm around Mamaw.

"And you're the biggest kid of the bunch. What kind of dastardly plan are you hatchin'?"

"Just fun. That's all. Fun."

Papaw finished up his cookie and brushed his hands together to get rid of the crumbs.

"Alrighty then, Kat, I'll leave you to it. Hunter, you're off the hook, buddy. Stay in here and keep these girls from gettin' into too much trouble. I think I'll go after those sandbags now. Be back in an hour or so."

Just as Papaw said that, it seemed that the whole sky opened up and threw down all the moisture it had been collecting. Rain, and possibly hail, pounded on the roof. Ruby gasped. The lights even flickered a bit.

"*Oooh*, we might have a blackout tonight!" Mamaw walked toward the pantry, opened the door, and disappeared for a minute. She soon backed out, holding a cardboard flat with several votive candles. "We better get ready!"

Great. This weather was not helping out with our initiation plans one bit.

"Here." Mamaw pointed to the candles in the flat. "Each of you take two and light them in all the rooms. If the lights go out later, it's gonna be too dark to even find a match."

She handed us some stick lighters, and we spread out to take them around the house.

"I feel much better now," Mamaw said. "You should have seen the last time the lights went out. I wasn't ready, and I bruised my shins on that dumb coffee table. I still have dents in the fronts of my legs!"

Thunder clapped, and Mamaw's little white dog with the cute black spots—Barney—appeared at my feet.

"Well, hello, Barn-Dog," I said, and I patted the back of his neck. "You afraid of a little storm?"

Mamaw shook her head. "He's been a scaredy-cat ever since Lucy ran away." Lucy was this stray dog that hung around with Barney so much I actually thought she was Mamaw's dog too. "He's so lonely, I was thinking of getting another dog."

"That would be fun," Lola said.

"Oh, check this out! I have a picture of a little mutt I saw at the shelter this morning." Mamaw took out her phone and scrolled her pictures to show us an adorable, white-haired puffball.

"She'll get pretty dirty if she lives out here," Lola said.

"Then you can come out and give her baths all the time," Mamaw said. "I really love her even more now looking at her picture again. I hope nobody's adopted her yet."

"I'm sure nobody's thinking of getting a new dog in the middle of this storm," I said. Then I got an idea.

"What are you gonna name her?"

Mamaw shrugged. "What do you think about Fifi? Or Snowball?"

I scrunched up my face. "Those names sound a little too . . . uh . . . fancy . . . for living out here in the country."

"But I like fancy names," Mamaw said.

"Okay then, how about choosing a fancy name that you

could shorten to sound spunky. Something like . . . Andrea." I shrugged. "You could call her Andi for short. Kind of like how everyone calls me Allie instead of Allison."

Kendall gasped.

I knew it was a risk to throw out the name Andi. But I *had* to do it.

I watched Mamaw's face closely for any kind of shock. Or sadness. Or . . . well, anything that would prove that she once had a son named Andy who got eaten by a gator.

But there was nothing but sheer joy.

"Andi, huh? That does sound spunky! And it rhymes with Candy and Handy and Dandy! I like it." Mamaw talked to the picture on the phone. "Okay, little Andi, you stay put now, until we can come and get you. I wish we could come now!"

For a minute I thought I'd encourage Mamaw to actually go out and get Andi so we could have the place to ourselves for the initiation, but that rain kept pelting down, and it was beginning to worry me a bit.

But then Mamaw's house phone rang.

"I'll get it!" Ruby ran to the phone. She's mesmerized by the thing that is attached to the wall with the long, stretchy cord.

"It's Aunt Janelle," Ruby said, and she practically ran all the way back to us with that long cord. She handed the receiver to Mamaw. "She sounds scared."

Mamaw scrunched her eyebrows, took the receiver from Ruby and held it to her ear. "Janelle, is everything okay?"

As Mamaw listened, she moved through the room, toward the coat closet. She pulled out a long raincoat and hat, and took her rain boots out of the closet while clamping that receiver between her chin and her shoulder.

"Now, honey, you listen to me. You're going to be okay, you understand? Take some deep breaths and relax. I'm on my way."

We girls froze in place and focused on Mamaw's every move.

"Janelle . . . Janelle?"

Mamaw ran to hang up the phone on the far wall, and then returned to the coat closet for an umbrella.

"Girls, Aunt Janelle slipped out on her porch. She doesn't think anything's broken, but she's having a panic attack or somethin'. I've gotta go over there."

My Great Aunt Janelle lives just up the road from my grand-parents' house, within walking distance. She's a little older than Mamaw, and much more of a worrier.

"I hope she's okay," Lola said.

"Can I come with you?" Hunter bolted from the cookie plate where he had been throwing down snickerdoodles and went for his raincoat.

Mamaw held her hands out. "No, dear, I want you to stay here and help the girls out with whatever they need. Papaw will be back shortly. If you kids need anything, call me on my cell, okay?"

We all nodded, wide-eyed. I wasn't happy that Aunt Janelle was suffering, but this was just the window of opportunity we needed.

As soon as the door closed behind Mamaw, Ruby pulled me aside.

"We have to do the frogs *now*—before they suffocate in that ice chest."

CHAPTER 18

Mud Slinging

Did I hear you say frogs?" Hunter plopped down on Papaw's overstuffed camo chair in the corner of the family room. "I like frogs."

I pulled the curtains open to look out on the fading daylight. Yes, the outside challenges would have to come first.

"Gather around, people. We have an initiation to conduct."

Kendall, Lola, and Ruby all sat down on Mamaw's brown cushy sofa with the sunflower throw pillows. Lola pulled a blanket around her shoulders and snuggled in.

"Don't get too comfortable," I said. "We're headed outside."

"In that freezing rain?" Lola whimpered. "Can't we do the singing first?"

"Frogs are dying," Ruby said, and she ran into the bedroom—I assumed to retrieve the ice chest.

"They'll be easier to catch if they're dead," Kendall said.

"Kendall!" Lola looked horrified. "How would you like to be suffocated in an ice chest?"

Ruby returned, with hope in her eyes and that beat-up ice chest in her hands.

"Wait," Hunter said. "I have to catch frogs that you brought with you? Were they in that ice chest in the back of the SUV?"

"Yes," I said. "Well, they were in there most of the time."

The girls and I all giggled.

"I don't get it," Hunter said.

"We'll fill you in later. For now, I need you to stand up so we can begin this Carroway Cousin Initiation."

Hunter popped up and stood straight, like he was a soldier about to be sworn into the military.

"Hunter Buster Carroway, today we will test the depth of your commitment to the family. How far will you go outside your comfort zone to prove that you are dedicated to cousin-hood? We, the Carroway girl cousins, hereby dedicate ourselves to your happiness and well-being, and to prove it, we promise to redo, redesign, rebuild, and even rename the Diva Duck Blind in the event that you complete four challenges put forth during this initiation. Do you promise to try your best, to not give up when things get rough, and to uphold the position of Carroway Cousin, no matter what the future holds?"

Hunter held his right hand up. "I do."

"I think he should put his other hand on the Bible," Kendall said.

I shook my head. "He's not becoming president. I think we can skip the Bible. Plus, doesn't it say somewhere in the Bible that you should just let your yes be yes and your no be no?"

"Yes," Ruby said. "That's what it says. It also says you should be kind to animals by not letting them die in ice chests ... or something like that."

"Okay then. Let's get on with challenge number one. Ruby, since this is the one you picked, you're in charge."

Ruby stepped forward—frog ice chest in hand—and turned toward the cousins.

"Hunter, challenge number one is going to be a little messy.

112

Since Carroways live in the bayou, we are confronted with the need to get muddy once in a while."

Hunter lowered his head and covered his face with his hands.

"Oh, no, not mud! I *hate* mud!"

"This we know," I said.

"But you can overcome it," Lola said. "It's only for a few minutes."

"Just until you catch the five bullfrogs that are hopefully still breathing in this ice chest." Ruby lifted the lid and a couple of them croaked. She sighed in relief.

"Okay," I said, taking charge again. "Everyone, follow me out to the mud hole behind the barn."

"But what will we tell Mamaw when she comes back and sees us all muddy?" Lola unzipped her backpack and snatched out one of her many beanies.

"We'll tell her we went out and played in the mud," I said. "Which is what we're actually going to be doing. Man, you people sure try to complicate things."

When we were all suited up in our rain clothes from the mudroom, Kendall opened the door which led out to the back of the house and the barn.

"I just want to remind you that damp weather is not at all good for my vocal chords."

As we stepped out into the rain, I remembered what Dr. Snow said—and I felt a surge of adrenaline in my stomach. I was supposed to stay inside, but that was impossible.

"Hey guys, I forgot something. I'll meet you out by the barn in one minute."

"Hurry, Allie," Ruby said. "The rain is letting up a little so we should start soon."

"Okay." The door closed behind them, and I ran to the bedroom to retrieve my pink mini-backpack—my "Allie-Kit." And now, in addition to the Epi-pen, it contained the brand-new asthma inhaler. The one I hadn't told the cousins about yet.

"When I say go, I will throw these frogs in the mud hole. Hunter, you can jump in at any time. When you catch one, yell over to me and I'll send one of the girls in to retrieve it and put it back in the ice chest."

"Wait, what?" Lola tucked her hair further into her beanie and stepped back from the mud hole. "I planned on just watching the madness, not getting involved."

"And I didn't bring a lot of clothes to change into," Kendall said.

Ruby stared at us, her hair frizzing and curling around her ears and forehead.

"We're *all* doing this, right Allie?"

"Of course." There was no getting out of this for me either. It would be hard to explain to my cousins now that the doctor had ordered me to stay warm and dry.

"Let's go before I freak out from mud anxiety," Hunter said.

Ruby smiled. "Okay, challenge number one. Starts. Now!"

She pulled the top off the ice chest, and poured the frogs into the hole. You could practically hear the joy in their croaks.

"Oh, no! They disappeared!" Hunter pushed his glasses up on his nose and then leaped into the hole after the frogs. He sank up to his hips in the mud.

"He's going to drown!" Lola yelled, and she knelt down next to the mud hole, which was about eight feet across.

"He'll be fine," I said. "It's not quicksand."

Hunter pushed both hands into the mud, which was more like a pool of muddy water now, with all the rain that had been pouring into it.

"That is just gross," Kendall said.

"Think about poor Hunter," Lola said.

"Hey, I think I have one!" Hunter sank down a little lower, mud up to his chest now. "Yeah. There you are, you little bugger. I can feel ya!"

Hunter swished his hands around a little more, and then, seconds later, they emerged from the mud holding a bullfrog. "One down, four to go!" Hunter yelled. And then he pulled in a deep breath and sank down to his neck in the mud. "Ooh, I think one is crawling up my leg!"

"As soon as you feel 'em, you gotta pounce on 'em!" Ruby jumped up and down and then into the hole to retrieve the first frog. Hunter handed it over and then sank back down to get the second frog.

That one emerged with a deafening croak—worse than one of Uncle Josiah's burps.

"That's so nasty," Lola said.

"Get in here and get him, Sis!" Ruby reached up, grabbed Lola by the arm, and pulled her in the hole.

"Hey! This isn't my challenge! I shouldn't have to . . ."

Lola started to spit and cough, because Ruby had thrown a fistful of mud in her face, splattering sloppy chunks into her mouth.

"Oh, you are so dead, Little Red!" Lola grabbed Ruby by the shoulders and shoved her down in the mud.

"I got him! Number three!" Hunter now held two frogs in the air.

"Kendall, can you get those frogs?" I pointed to the two sisters who were wrestling around in the mud. "Ruby and Lola are busy."

Kendall shook her head and grabbed at her leather choker, which had to be shrinking up in the rain and, well, choking her.

"I'd really prefer to . . ."

She didn't get a chance to say what she'd prefer, because I moved over and pushed her into the hole with the rest of the cousins.

"You ladies are clogging up my frog hunt!" Hunter said, passing off the two frogs to Kendall. And then he dove over to the other side of the hole after something. "Got you! Number four!"

He held the biggest of the frogs up in the air. "This one has some meaty legs!"

About all I could see of Hunter, besides mud, was his smiling, white teeth.

"Put him in the ice chest," I yelled, but no one could hear me over the squeals and screams and the fighting.

"Don't make me come in there. I'm not supposed to . . ."

And then a muddy hand reached up, grabbed me, and pulled me in with the rest of the bunch. I'm not sure whose hand it was. At this point, everyone just looked like a mud monster.

"Oh, no! There he goes! Don't let him get away!" Hunter's voice rang out over the laughing, squealing, and croaking.

We all froze and looked in the direction Hunter was

pointing. The fifth frog had escaped the hole somehow and started hopping merrily away from us.

"Come back!" Hunter tried to climb out of the hole and follow the frog, but by the time he got out and on his feet, the croaking fellow was long gone.

"Noooooo!" Hunter dashed forward, into the new torrent of rain coming from the sky. Lola, Ruby, Kendall, and I, still stuck in the hole, watched the drama unfold.

"C'mon, Hunter! You can do it! Catch that thing!" Kendall shouted over the rain and other commotion.

Hunter disappeared from our view, and we all grew silent. We pulled ourselves from the hole and tried to wash some of the mud off with the rain.

"I can't believe you pulled me in," Lola said to Ruby.

"I can't believe you pushed me in," Kendall said to me.

"I can't believe I'm outside," I said, under my breath. I *hope I haven't made a terrible mistake.*

We waited another minute for any word from Hunter.

Finally, he trudged back into our view, his head hanging and shoulders slumped.

"He got away. I'll never find him."

I was stumped for what to do next. The challenge was for him to catch all five frogs. The boy had been a trooper and had done more than I ever thought he would, given the severity of that mud. As far as I was concerned, he had passed the test.

"I told you I'd fail, Allie!"

We all just stood there in a circle and stared at each other.

"Well, we kinda got in your way in the mud hole," Lola said. "Sorry about that, cousin."

"Yeah, we got a little carried away," Ruby said.

"Carried Away with the Carroways," Hunter said.

We all laughed.

"My choker is seriously choking me," Kendall said. "Can we get out of this mess? Maybe you'll catch that dumb frog during the hunting challenge."

"Hunting challenge?" Hunter glanced at me and Lola, his eyes wide. "You're gonna make me hunt?"

"It's what all Carroways do," Kendall said, and she pointed her index finger at him. "And you gotta cook it too." Then she took off toward Mamaw's house, pulling her choker away from her throat.

Hunter just stood there, dripping and shaking his head.

"I'm doomed," he said.

"No, you're not." Lola patted him on the back and then began to pull him with us as we walked toward the house. "You're gonna do just fine. You're not going to use a gun. Your slingshot should be able to take down a squirrel, no problem."

"I gotta cook a squirrel? How do I do that?"

"Just roast it on a stick," Lola said. "No one said we had to eat it. It just needs to be cooked."

"I think you should skin and clean it first," Ruby said. "Squirrel is actually pretty tasty."

"That's so disgusting," I shivered.

So did Hunter. Thankfully, we were almost to the house, where we could dry off, warm up, and prepare for the next challenge.

Unfortunately, when I got back inside I realized that my Allie-Kit was missing.

CHAPTER 19

Challenge Two

The last thing I remembered was pulling the straps onto my wrist when I left the house. But how long was it there before it fell off? Did I have it on when Ruby threw the frogs in the mud hole? It was all a confusing blur.

"I call shower first!" Kendall pulled her rain boots off in the mudroom and shoved them under the wooden bench.

"Why are you taking a shower?" Ruby stood there, dripping. "We're not done with the challenges yet."

Kendall put both hands on her hips. "*My* challenge takes place indoors. Plus, I just want the mud off now!"

"Me too," Hunter said. "I'll go rinse off outside with the hose." He went out the door toward the spigot near the fish-gutting table.

"Sounds freezing." Lola shivered, grabbed a towel, and wrapped her hair up in it.

"Guys, I think I have to go back out there for a minute."

Just as I said that, another downpour began. And then the lights flickered.

"Never mind."

Hunter came running back in.

"Then again," he said. "A towel's just as good."

"We better do the hunting before the river rises even more."

Ruby pointed down the walk from my grandparents' house. The water was all the way up to the mailbox.

"Whoa!" Lola gasped. "Should we pull the kayak out from under the house?"

I stared out toward the river, wondering if my Allie-Kit was floating down it.

"I'm calling Mamaw," I said. "I wonder if she realizes that the river has risen so high?"

"Where's Papaw?" Hunter looked out the window. "Shouldn't he be back with those sandbags by now?"

I ran to the wall phone, still dripping a little, and dialed Aunt Janelle's number, which was listed on the whiteboard in the kitchen. It rang and rang and rang.

"Try Mamaw's cell," Ruby said, as she wrung her braid out with a towel.

I knew that number by heart. It went right to voicemail.

I shook my head and hung up. "Nothing."

"How about Papaw?" Hunter asked. "Can you call *him*?"

I frowned and shook my head. "He only turns his phone on if he's going to call someone."

"You should call your parents," Lola said.

No chance. Not till I find my Allie-Kit.

"Nope. We're perfectly fine. I'm sure the rain will let up soon, but let's pull the kayak out and get it up on the porch. Just in case."

All of us—except Kendall, who was singing her lungs out in the shower—bundled up again and ran for the area under the house where all the "boats" are stored. Most of the "boats" didn't float anymore, but the red tandem ocean kayak was brand-new.

"Don't forget to grab the seats and paddles," I said. "When I count to three, we'll lift and carry it up onto the porch."

Hunter bent down to grab a handle on the nose of the kayak. "Why exactly are we doing this?"

"In case we have to escape," I said. "Don't you watch the news during Louisiana floods?"

"Yeah," Ruby said. "Everyone loads their family and pets in boats, and then they paddle themselves to higher ground."

"Okay, everyone!" I yelled. "One, two, three!"

Hunter and I lifted from the handles on each end. Lola lifted her side a little too fast, which flipped the kayak upside down, spilling all the contents into the mud.

I stood up straight and jammed my hands on my hips.

"This would never cut it in a real emergency, people. Let's try that again."

We flipped the kayak back upright, piled the muddy seats and paddles in, and lifted. Then we trudged toward the house, pushed and pulled awkwardly up the stairs to the porch, and set the kayak down.

"This thing is long," Hunter said.

"That's good," I said. "It will hold all of us, and the Barn-Dog."

"Where *is* Barney?" Hunter brushed new mud off the sides of his shorts and scanned the soggy landscape for signs of Mamaw's goofy dog. "I could use him to help me hunt."

Just then, Kendall emerged from the front door, looking all peaceful and mud-free.

"Are we going to start challenge two? We don't have much time before it gets dark."

I looked at Lola and raised my eyebrows. Challenge two

was hers to conduct. She disappeared inside for a minute and came out with a slingshot. She handed it to Hunter.

"Hunter Carroway, you have already proven that you can hunt doves when everyone is helping you during the TV show. But now you must show that you have what it takes to live off the land. As God intended."

"Oh, really? Then why did he give us grocery stores, huh?" Hunter flashed his witty grin, but it wasn't going to get him out of this.

Lola continued, "Dad calls the land out here God's grocery store. If you're gonna survive as a Carroway, you better get used to huntin', guttin', and then eatin' whatever you find out here."

I scrunched up my face. I've been a Carroway since day one, and I still can't stand the look, smell, or feel of animal guts.

"So where am I supposed to go?" Hunter turned and looked out from the porch, and as he did, the rain tapered off to a heavy mist.

"I think he should have a buddy," Ruby said.

Kendall smoothed her clean, wet hair behind her ears. "Don't look at me."

I thought about my lost emergency kit—something I needed to hunt down before the wheezes came back.

"I'll go with him."

"Are you sure?" Lola looked relieved.

"Yeah. C'mon, Hunter. Let's go get some food."

"How much time do we have?" Hunter asked.

"As long as it takes," Lola said.

"Or until you give up," Kendall added.

Lola gave her the stink-eye.

"Just come back with something to cook. Squirrel, lizard, snake, frog, duck . . . it doesn't matter."

The screen door slammed behind us, and Hunter and I made our way down the stairs.

"Frog, huh? If we could find that one that got away, do you think they would count that for this challenge too?"

"I doubt it," I said. "Kendall's not interested in redesigning the Diva. You don't want to give her any loopholes."

Hunter nodded, loaded his sling with a big rock, and focused his eyes on the ground.

"What animals do you think are still out here in this weather?"

I thought about the only living things I knew that were stubborn enough to still be out.

Gators. And Carroways.

A familiar tightness gripped my chest. I stopped a minute, breathed in, and then blew out.

"You okay?" Hunter stopped but didn't look back.

I breathed in again, and on the breath out, my lungs turned wheezy.

Great.

"Allie? What is it?"

Hunter asked, his face still focused forward.

I grabbed my throat.

"I'm, uh . . . having a little trouble breathing."

Hunter stopped walking and turned toward me.

"Are you having another asthma attack? Didn't you see the doctor today?"

He stared at me with those transparent green eyes.

Might as well tell him.

"Come with me." I grabbed his elbow and led him back to the barn and under the eaves for cover. "Hunter, when we were all wrestling in the frog hole, did you notice a pink mini backpack attached to me anywhere?"

Hunter looked out and scanned the hole.

"I don't know. I wasn't really focused on you. I was busy freaking out about the mud."

"Did you notice if I had it when we were walking back to the house? Have you seen it on me at all?"

Hunter shrugged. "Sorry, Allie. I haven't."

I bent over, put my hands on my knees, and breathed in.

"That's okay. It's just that the doctor gave me an inhaler to use when I get short of breath. It's in that backpack. And . . ."

I stopped to breathe.

"And, what?" Hunter laid the slingshot down on the ground, and bent down, close to my face.

"And, I guess I lost it."

"Oh no, Allie. What are we going to do?"

"Well, it has to be somewhere between here and the house. I remember going to get it when we were leaving for the challenge. But then things got all muddy."

"Then that's what we need to hunt for right now. You're turning purple around your lips and eyes."

"I am?" I put my hands up to my cheeks. "I'm not supposed to be out here in the damp weather. Doctor's orders."

"Then *why* are you out here?"

"You needed a hunting buddy."

Hunter started to pace back and forth, under the eaves.

"You're really stubborn, you know that?"

"I'm a Carroway. It runs in the family."

Hunter pulled his jacket off and threw it around me like a blanket. "Sit down here and don't move. If there's a pink backpack out there, I'll find it."

The sun had still not set, but it was getting close, and things were dark anyway because of the rainclouds. So, when Hunter got a little ways away from me, I could barely see him.

A furry rodent scurried right in front of me.

"Squirrel!" I yelled.

Hunter came running back into view.

"What? Allie, are you okay?"

"Yes! There's a squirrel!" I pointed to it as it leaped away from me.

Hunter jumped up and down in the mud.

"Seriously, Allie? I'm on a more important mission right now, don't you think?"

He looked hilarious, all wide-eyed and drenched. I started to laugh a little.

"Oh. Sorry."

But then there was another one.

"*Squirrel*! Get it Hunter!" I picked up the slingshot and held it out to Hunter.

"Quick! You need it to pass this challenge!"

"Allie! I don't care about the challenge right now!"

Hunter turned and ran away. I thought about trying to get the squirrel myself, but I felt too winded, not to mention that would have been cheating. So I just sat there, under the barn eaves, watching the rain roll off the roof and carve divots in the wet earth in front of me. I prayed for Hunter's safety and that somewhere out there he would find my Allie-Kit with the magic inhaler.

It seemed like at least thirty minutes went by before I saw Hunter again. Thankfully the rain had let up a bit, and I had formed a comfortable heat bubble under his jacket as I sat on the ground with my back leaning against the barn wall. I might have even fallen asleep for a few minutes.

Hunter dragged himself up the hill to the barn. I'd never seen him with such a sad face.

He sat down next to me and hung his head.

"It's not out there, Allie. I searched every square foot between the barn and the house. I dug through the mud and everything. I'm so sorry." He held out his dirty hands. He really did look like a mud monster. Again.

For some reason, seeing his desperation made me want to cry.

"That's okay. It means a lot that you tried."

Hunter shivered. "I'm freezing," he said.

"You haven't had your jacket. Here." I took off the jacket and handed it to him. Then I stood up and picked up the slingshot.

"We should get back to the house."

Hunter shook his head. "But I don't have anything to cook."

I smiled and handed him the slingshot.

"Maybe those squirrels will return before we get there."

CHAPTER 20

Blend

The squirrels didn't return.

Defeated and cold, we cleaned up as best we could and stepped from the mudroom into the family room.

"Finally!" Kendall sat at the kitchen counter, drinking something hot. "What did y'all catch?"

"Possible pneumonia," I said. "The animals all went home in the crazy weather, so we decided to do the same. We'll try later."

"So what you're saying is that Hunter is zero for two? Looks like we get to keep the Diva." She smirked and took another sip of her drink. "It's okay, Brother, I still love ya." She winked at Hunter.

"The night's not over yet," Hunter said. "I'll catch that fifth frog, and I'll find something we can cook, you'll see."

"I like the stubbornness," Lola said.

"He sounds like a Carroway," Ruby added.

"Oh, really?" Kendall put her drink down, went out to the family room, and grabbed her phone. "But can the boy sing?"

She scrolled through her screen, then held the phone up toward us.

"Hunter, it's time for challenge number three in our Carroway Cousin Initiation. You need to prove that you can carry a tune by singing with our quartet. There's a lot of music that happens in the Diva Duck Blind, so if you're going to be up there with us, you have to learn how to blend."

A song started to play, but the sound was immediately drowned out by another thunder clap and a new cloudburst pounding down on the roof.

Then the lights went off.

"Blackout!" Ruby yelled.

Thankfully, the candles we lit earlier were still burning, so as soon as our eyes adjusted, we could see a few things.

"Where are Mamaw and Papaw?" Lola sat on the sofa and pulled her blanket tighter around her shoulders. "Do you think they're all right? Should we call Mamaw again?"

"Maybe," I said. "But I gotta dry off first."

"Me too," Hunter said. "And I think I need some hot tea or something before I try this 'blending' thing you're talking about. I might even have to protest this challenge given that I am a pre-adolescent male in the middle of a voice change."

"You could try yodeling," Ruby said.

"Oh, please," Kendall said. "Don't be givin' him any crazy ideas."

"Yodeling is singing," I said.

"But it has to *sound* good," Kendall said. "I refuse to pass him on this challenge unless we sound good."

"Okay, just give me a minute to get into some performance clothes for my singing debut." Hunter bowed, then walked over to me and whispered in my ear. "Don't worry. You warned me about this, so I came up with a plan."

And then he disappeared into the bedroom.

Ruby picked out some wood pieces from the steel box next to the fireplace and threw a few logs in. Then she found a stick lighter and flicked it on as she turned the gas key on the wall.

"This will give us more light, plus warm us all up. Allie, you should change and then get over here. You don't look so good."

It must be serious if she can tell I don't look right even in the dark.

"Yeah," Kendall added. "And we have to show you the new 'Andy evidence' that we found while you were outside gettin' drenched."

"It's disturbing, Allie." Lola pulled a purple crocheted blanket from the sofa and brought it over to me. "You're gonna want to change your challenge when you see it."

I took the blanket and wrapped up in it. It felt so good, but I did wonder if my eyes and lips matched the deep lavender shade. I looked around at my cousins. Three level-headed, intelligent girls most of the time. Why did this Andy thing freak them out so badly?

"It's a camp story, girls. That's all. I'm sure there's a good explanation for whatever you found."

"I'm ready!" Hunter burst out of the bedroom, and walked toward Kendall with a full-on swagger. He wore oversized light-gray sweatpants, that were bunched up at the bottom inside some black high-top tennis shoes, a white T-shirt, and a huge red hoodie. With the hood on his head.

"What do you think you're doin'?" Kendall tried to keep a straight face, but it was hard, even for her.

The rest of us girls giggled.

"We gonna start this thang or what? And don't worry. I ain't yodelin'," Then he crossed his arms up high in front of himself, like a rapper posing for his CD cover.

"Oh, boy. This is gonna be good." Lola popped up off the sofa. "What are we singing?"

"Can I pick the song?" Hunter's eyes gleamed, even in the firelight.

"Yes," Kendall said. "But it has to be spiritual."

"Not a problem," Hunter said. "I pick that old hymn called 'Nothin' but the Blood of Jesus.'"

"Seriously?" Kendall began to scroll on her phone. "I'm surprised you even know that song."

"Oh, I know it, all right. Plus, I want to rock it. With no background music." He walked over to Kendall, took her phone from her hand, and placed in on the coffee table.

"Excuse me? Rock it?" She put her hand on one hip and flipped her hair with the other. "Exactly how do you intend to 'rock it?'"

"Don't you worry, sister. I got this. Now just give me a count to get started. And don't make it too slow and boring. When you girls catch on, you can join in."

I could hardly believe what I was hearing. Either Hunter really knew what he was doing, or he had gone crazy-mad from too much mud on the brain.

Kendall just stared at him for a moment. Then she shook her head.

"Okay, it's your challenge to lose. Come on, girls. Let's line up in front of the fire. Pretend we've got an audience."

We did what she asked, and I closed my eyes just for a second to pray for Hunter.

I like to root for underdogs.

As I prayed, I heard Kendall count . . . "One, two, three, *four!*"

And I could *not* believe what I heard next.

CHAPTER 21

You Call that Singin'?

It was drums.

No. It wasn't drums. There were no drums anywhere in the room.

We all stared at Hunter.

He held his hands up in the air.

"How come you aren't singing? I'm giving you percussion!"

Then the drums started up again.

Hunter was beatboxing.

All our mouths hung wide open.

"What's wrong, girls? Did you forget the words? Let me help. What can wash away my sin?"

Then he made some drumbeat noises with his hands and cheeks. We just kept staring.

"Oh, come on! Nothing but the blood of Jesus? Singers, keep up."

He continued, beating and boxing, tapping his foot, and staring at us, until Kendall finally shrugged and began singing.

"What can make me whole again?"

Ruby, Lola, and I echoed. "Nothing but the blood of Jesus."

The rest was Carroway history, although no one was recording it. We rocked the whole first verse and chorus, like we had practiced it for weeks. Lola and Ruby even started a little dance action. I didn't even try to join them, since I have no dancing talent, whatsoever. My coordination stops at flips and cartwheels.

The fire crackled hot behind us. By the time we finished our song, I was sweating and had thrown the purple blanket off. I didn't know whether to laugh or cry. The whole situation was hilarious—a perfect mix of Carroway weirdness.

The best thing was I could finally breathe a little.

"Congratulations, Hunter! I think you got this one!" Ruby plopped down on the sofa and bounced up and down.

"*Where* did you learn to beatbox?" Lola crumbled to the ground, laughing and grabbing her stomach.

Hunter smiled and then shuffled his feet in a little break-dance move. "My first foster family was into hip-hop."

"Oh, man, that's the *best*!" Lola rolled around on the floor and laughed some more. "Do it again."

Hunter rattled off a snare and a kick.

"Can you show me how to do that?" Ruby stared at Hunter's mouth, and she raised her hands to her lips and blew out something that sounded like a broken duck call.

"Stop." Kendall held her hand out. "Just stop right now." She looked at Hunter. "You call that singin'?"

Hunter dropped his hands to his sides, and I think I saw his shoulders droop, even inside that baggy hoodie.

"It's music. And I blended, right?"

"Kendall," I said. "I think we sounded better than ever. You gotta give him this one."

"Yeah, Kendall. The group is better now with Hunter." Ruby twisted that red braid around and around.

I watched Kendall's eyes search our faces.

"I'll think about it," she said. "It was *my* challenge, after all, and I did say that you had to *sing*. Beatboxing, while clever and fun, is not singin'."

Hunter shrugged. "Okay, whatever you say. I guess I'll change back into my regularly-scheduled "loser" clothes, then. I'll be right back."

He formed an "L" on his forehead with his hand and slumped back into the bedroom.

Lola jumped up from the floor and got in Kendall's face.

"That was mean, Kendall! He did great and you know it. Did you see how he walked out of here? Is that how you plan to treat him once he's officially your brother? Maybe he *would* be better off with a different family."

"Lola!" Ruby came off the couch and pulled her sister away from Kendall.

"Okay—that's enough, people." I walked over to the cousins, who had gotten carried away—yet again. I sat each one down on a different piece of furniture and stood in the middle of them.

"Come on! We're not going to fight over a stupid initiation." I stared at each one. "Take a deep breath and count to ten. I would if I could do it without wheezing."

That got them to grin a little.

"Well, I guess he did kind of blow me away with his hidden talent," Kendall said.

"And I guess it's true, he didn't actually sing, and that was the challenge." Lola looked down at the floor. "Kendall, I'm sorry I said what I said."

"It's okay." Kendall fiddled with her choker. "I really want Hunter to do well, I just don't want to lose the Diva."

"That's totally understandable," Ruby said.

"Yeah. Changes are hard," Lola agreed.

We needed some help here.

"Where's Mamaw's Bible? I think we need to remember why we started all this in the first place." I walked around the family room and kitchen area, searching for the faded leather Bible with the broken binding. Mamaw keeps a rubber band around it so the pages don't spill out when she carries it to church.

"Ah, here it is." It was sitting over on the kitchen counter, right next to the recipe box. Mamaw is known to read Scripture verses while she waits for yeast to rise when she makes bread.

I carefully moved the Bible to the center island and took off the rubber band. Kendall, Lola, and Ruby circled around as I turned to the book of Romans.

"Mamaw sure writes a lot in her Bible," Lola said.

It's true. You can barely see any white space for all the notes written in the margins. She's got dates, and underlines, and even pictures drawn in some places. Mamaw says she'll never get a new Bible because of all the valuable memories in this one.

I located Romans 12:9–10 and began to read:

"Don't just pretend to love others. Really love them. Hate what is wrong. Hold tightly to what is good. Love each other with genuine affection, and take delight in honoring each other."

I stared at the words, and for some reason, my thoughts didn't go to Hunter this time. They went to my parents.

Could this be why my parents were considering moving? Could they love me that much? Could they take delight in living in cactusville because it would honor me? Could I sacrifice like that for someone I loved?

Ruby gasped. "Allie! Look!"

Ruby's shaking index finger pointed just inside the margin by verse nine.

"Holy Gator Busters!" Kendall stepped back and grabbed her forehead. "There's your proof! We can't send him into that shed now."

I stared down at the single word that Mamaw had penned in her Bible, right next to Romans, chapter twelve.

It said . . . Andy.

CHAPTER 22

Long, Lost Uncle?

I was speechless. Why was the name Andy scribbled in Mamaw's Bible? There had to be a better explanation than having a son who got eaten by an alligator.

Right?

Kendall ran to the end table by the recliner in the family room. She grabbed what looked like an old photo album and brought it over to the kitchen island.

"We found this while you were out huntin'." She opened the stiff cover to reveal the first page that held decorative letters that spelled out "Carroway Family Reunion." The sticky pages behind the letters had yellowed a bit, and the pictures on the next few pages were mostly black and white mixed in with a few faded-out color ones.

"See anyone you recognize?" Kendall set both elbows on the island and rested her chin in her hands. "Here, I'll help you out. There's Papaw Ray." She pointed to a much younger looking version of Papaw. He kind of looked like my dad.

"And there's Mamaw." Lola pointed to the stylish and smiling dark-haired woman standing next to our tall, rugged, camo-wearing Papaw.

"We think that's Aunt Janelle, but who knows for sure, it's so fuzzy." Kendall swept her finger over a lady's face in the back row of adults who were outnumbered by a bunch of kids in the front. "And the kids must be our dads, and some cousins, nieces, and nephews or something."

"There sure are lots of boys," I said. "Funny how we have mostly girl kids in the family now."

"Yeah," Kendall said. "Count 'em."

There were eleven.

"I have no idea who they all are, do you?" I looked real close, and I picked out the most familiar looking face. "Is that my dad? He looks like Papaw Ray a little bit."

Lola nodded. "We think so. And if that's true, then the other four boys standing around him must be brothers. See how all the kids in the picture are all bunched in separate groups?"

"But that would make five," I said. "That's one too many."

"Exactly," Kendall said. "And that proves it. One of these boys is our long-lost Uncle Andy."

"I think this one is him." Ruby pointed to a kid who looked to be about ten. "He's got reddish hair. That's where I must have gotten it."

"This had to be just a couple of years before he got eaten." Kendall hung her head. "It's so sad that we never got to meet him."

I think I heard Lola sniff. "Lola, are you crying? Really?"

Lola reached out, grabbed a tissue out of a box on the island and pulled it to her nose.

"This kid could be anybody. And I don't think that's red hair, Ruby. I think it's an ink smudge, or spaghetti sauce." I rubbed my finger over the picture.

"Don't smear his face!" Kendall pulled the book toward her. "That could be the only image we have left of him!"

"People, get a grip. I need to see more evidence than just a faded face on an old picture and a name written in a Bible."

"We should look him up on the Internet. Maybe there's a newspaper article about what happened." For being the youngest, Ruby sure lends common sense to the group sometimes.

"I've never thought of that," Kendall said.

"Me either." I crossed my arms. "Because the whole thing's baloney."

Lola, Kendall, and Ruby all shot out to the family room after their phones.

"Mine's dead," Kendall said.

"Mine's not getting coverage." Lola shook her phone.

"Same here," Ruby said. "No bars at all."

I decided to check mine. Same thing.

"I'm sure it has to do with the storm. Maybe the cell tower's down. No biggie."

"I don't like this at all." Lola went for her blanket again. "We're out here all by ourselves with no grownups. And the water's rising."

Just then, the door to the bedroom flew open and a clean, less hip-hoppy twelve-year-old Carroway boy emerged.

"Still no grown-ups? That's a good thing, right? Now we can finish this initiation off in epic fashion. What's challenge number four?"

CHAPTER 23

To Shed or Not to Shed

Epic would be if we could put an end to the Andy horror story forever. And all Hunter needed to do was to survive being in that dumb shed for an hour.

He could do it. I was sure of it.

Well, mostly sure. I would have been more sure if I hadn't seen that reunion picture and the name in the Bible.

"I'm ready." Hunter held his hands up in the air. "That shower made me feel like a new man. I'm ready to win this challenge and find a way to pass the other ones too. The Diva is going down, cousins."

Kendall stared me down across the room. "Allie, can we talk in the other room?"

She didn't give me a chance to say yes or no, she just pulled me by the elbow back into Mamaw and Papaw's bedroom.

"You *have* to change the challenge. We can't send him in that shed. Not with all the new information we just found. I don't want to be responsible for losing Hunter before we get a chance to adopt him."

Kendall paced back and forth, adjusting her choker. The thunder and lightning started up outside and more rain and wind beat against the house. The one little candle on Mamaw's nightstand cast huge Kendall shadows on the wall.

"Well, what do you say? Can we think of another challenge? Allie?"

"We *could* think of one . . ." I went over and picked up the candle. "But it wouldn't be epic." I walked over to Mamaw's dresser, where she had crowded every square inch with framed photos of our family. I shined the candle close to a few of the pictures of our dads when they were little. "Check these out, Kendall. They look like they were taken around the same time as those other pictures, but there's no little red-haired boy anywhere."

Kendall joined me to look. "Maybe they got rid of the ones with Andy so they wouldn't be sad when they saw them."

"That doesn't make any sense. Mamaw and Papaw would want to remember if he was their kid. Plus, this family would never make a spooky camp story out of a family tragedy. I think all the drama with the storm tonight is impairing your judgment."

Kendall sat down on the bed and sighed.

"Maybe you're right. But can't we just make up a different challenge anyway? I'm sure we would all feel more comfortable that way."

I replaced the candle on the nightstand. Then I went over and put my hand on Kendall's shoulder.

"This initiation is not about comfort. You think anything we've done tonight has been comfortable for Hunter? Think about the mud. He's been in mud since we got here—and he hates it! But did you see his face out there? He's proud. The boy deserves to finish out with something epic. He might have failed the last three challenges, but sitting in a dark shed for an hour is something he can actually do. After he comes out, we'll tell him the story about the gator, and then he'll be extra proud."

Kendall looked at me with wide eyes.

"It's gonna be great. You'll see."

This time I grabbed Kendall by the elbow and led her out of the bedroom and into the family room, where Hunter, Ruby, and Lola were drinking hot cocoa.

"Is something wrong?" Lola asked. "I mean, besides the fact that Mamaw and Papaw have disappeared, the river is rising, and we don't have power."

"Nothing's wrong," I said. "We were just discussing the final challenge." I turned to face Hunter. "I hope you are feeling brave, kid, because this one is going to be a little scary."

Hunter drained the last of the hot cocoa out of his mug and stood up straight.

"I'm ready."

"Okay then." I walked over in front of the fire and began the explanation. "Hunter, there's a place on this property that scares the wits out of most everyone in the family."

"Are you talking about the haunted shed?" The spooky way Hunter said that, mixed with the candlelight in the room gave me goosebumps.

"Hunter, you know about that?" Ruby stared in my direction.

"Only that there's a lot of weird noises, and people don't like going in there. But it's not a problem. I don't believe in ghosts."

"Well, that's a good thing," I said. "Because challenge four—the final test of your Carroway Cousin fortitude—requires you to stay in the haunted shed for one hour."

Hunter held his open hands toward the ceiling.

"That's it?"

"Almost. You also can't have any lights."

"So, in the dark, then?"

"Yeah." I was puzzled as to why he was smiling.

"Cool. I can do that. When do I start?"

"Better be soon." Lola, who had been standing over by the window, gestured to the view outside. "The river is up to the bench now."

The bench is Mamaw's prayer bench, which is about five feet from the stairs leading up to the house. I only remembered one time when the water got that high.

"It's okay," I said. "There's no way the water is going to make it up the hill to where the shed is."

"He needs a coat and a blanket. There's not going to be any heat in there." Lola pulled out a couple of blankets from the hall closet. "And I strongly suggest he have some way to protect himself."

"From what?" Hunter asked. "A bunch of stuffed animal heads, some rusted tools, and boxes of junk? I'll be fine"

"You can take the slingshot," I said.

"Hey, maybe I'll hunt down a raccoon or something. Can you cook a raccoon? Can I bring my duct tape? That stuff comes in handy."

I shrugged. "That's fine with me."

Hunter made his way out to the mudroom with his slingshot and the roll of duct tape. We all put our coats and boots back on and followed Hunter out the door. Lola lugged the blankets.

"It's this way, right?" Hunter pointed up the hill, past the barn where I sat while Hunter looked for my Allie-Kit.

"Yeah, that building up to the left." I pointed my headlamp toward the large, rickety shed in the distance. I thought I heard a groan the minute my light beam fell on it.

"I hope it's not locked," Lola said.

I laughed.

"Are you kidding? A burglar would be doing this family a favor by coming and taking everything out of that shed. Stuff in there has to be fifty years old."

We approached the door. Ruby stepped forward to pry it open. The loud, long creaking sound was worse than finger-nails on a chalkboard. We all covered our ears.

"Oh, good," Kendall said. "I think I just went deaf."

Ruby shined her headlamp into the dark entrance. "Hellooooo in there!"

Lola grabbed the back of Ruby's shoulder. "Why did you just do that? What if someone . . . or something . . . is in there? You want them to hear you?"

The thunder clapped, and we all jumped.

Hunter pushed the girls away from the opening. "Like I said, there's nothing in there but stuffed heads, rusted tools, and boxes of junk. And now, me." Hunter slapped his chest. "I'm goin' in. See y'all in sixty minutes."

He grabbed one blanket from Lola and turned to face the blackness.

"Keep your slingshot loaded," I said as I patted him on the back. He gave me a funny look.

"You know, in case of raccoons. Or squirrels." I winked.

Hunter smiled.

And then he disappeared.

"Should we shut the door?" Ruby grabbed the doorknob.

"NO!" Lola was white as a ghost. "What if it gets stuck, and the gator is in there, and Hunter can't get out? Leave it open."

"Yes," Kendall said. "Leave it open. My ears can't take much more assault."

We all stood there, staring at each other.

"What should we do now?" Ruby asked.

Then we heard it. A loud groan that sent shivers up my spine.

"GOOOOOO BAAACK TO THE HOUUUUUUSE!"

Hunter.

Just maybe he was going to get the best of us yet.

CHAPTER 24

Waiting and Wondering

"Now what?" Lola grabbed her blanket again after we all had taken our wet coats and boots off in the mudroom.

"We need something to take our minds off what's going on in that shed," I said.

"Kendall and Ruby, go gather all the candles in the house and bring them to the kitchen island so we have as much light as possible. Lola, help me bring all those albums over. If there are more pictures of this mystery boy, I want to find them."

The girls hopped into action, and in minutes we were poring over more faded pictures in Mamaw's photo albums.

"Check this one out!" Ruby pulled one book over so we could all see it. "There's a section for each of our dads."

The pictures weren't very good quality—a lot were out of focus—and most of them were of the same thing—a different boy holding up a fish he had caught or a string of ducks after a successful hunting trip. There were a few of each boy swimming in the river, and a couple of them eating bowls of gumbo that Mamaw probably cooked.

"Hmm," Ruby said. "Not much has changed for our dads. They still do all this stuff."

"Only now they make us do it too," I said.

"I think it's pretty fun." Ruby smiled, flipping through the old albums.

"I prefer to sing," Kendall said.

"And I hate wearing camo," Lola added.

"But all in all, we have a pretty nice family." I closed one photo album and opened another. "I can't imagine myself living with any other types of people."

"Me neither." Kendall smoothed her hand over a picture of her dad.

"Here! I found him again! The red-haired kid!" Ruby lowered her face closer to a photo in the middle of one of the pages. "Yep, that's him alright! He's standing next to a tent."

I grabbed the album and pulled it over to look at it.

"That's some weird kind of tent. Are you sure that's the same kid?"

"Let's compare!" Kendall opened the other album and pulled the crumbling plastic cover open to release the picture. She lifted it off the sticky page and placed it next to the kid by the tent.

"Pictures were such bad quality in the old days," Lola said. "What is that picture on the tent?"

"It looks like fruit in a cornucopia." Ruby laughed.

"Let's see if we can find any more pictures of him." Lola pulled another album off the stack of about six.

"I'm gonna look in Mamaw's Bible. Maybe she wrote Andy's name somewhere else."

"Good idea, Kendall." I don't know why I was encouraging her, but I did want to solve this mystery. "Start looking in the book of Psalms, in all the parts where David is sad or mad. If I lost a son, I'd be reading and writing in those places."

Kendall cracked the Bible open right in the middle, and flipped a little to the left to find Psalms.

"You can barely see the Bible words with all of Mamaw's underlinin' and notes." Kendall used her pointer finger and scanned page after page looking for Andy's name.

"Found another one!" Ruby ripped open the plastic, pulled out another picture, and set it by the others. "Some other boy has him in a headlock."

We all gathered around the picture.

"Is that Uncle Adam?" I picked up the photo and held it close to a candle. Uncle Adam is the oldest of the Carroway brothers. My dad is next, then Kendall's dad, Wayne, then Ruby and Lola's dad, Josiah. If there really was an Andy—he must have fallen somewhere in the middle.

"Mamaw could have made this much easier by labeling these pictures." Lola squinted as she studied the pages of another album.

"I'm pretty sure she saved all her pen ink for this Bible," Kendall said. "My eyes are startin' to hurt."

Just then, the phone on the wall rang, and we all jumped.

"Don't answer it," Lola said. "We're in the middle of a big discovery here."

"But it could be Mamaw. What if she's hurt or stuck somewhere?" I went for the phone.

"Hello?" I prayed it wouldn't be my mom or dad asking how my inhaler and I were getting along.

"Allie-girl! It's so good to hear your voice. How're y'all doin' down there?"

Mamaw.

Whew.

"Mamaw? Are you alright? How's Aunt Janelle?"

I watched as my cousins relaxed and went right back to scanning albums and Bibles.

"Oh, she's a little shook up, and she has a migraine headache, but I gave her some medicine and put her to bed. I tried to come on back to the house, but the water is right up to the door. Is Papaw back with those sandbags yet?"

"He never came back, Mamaw."

"Oh, you poor dears! I bet they closed the road to town and he can't get back. Did you try callin' him?" Mamaw laughed. "Never mind what I just said. He never has his phone on. Oh, my, are you kids okay? The lights are off here."

"Yeah, they're off here too. But we have the candles."

"I'm so sorry you're alone."

"We're not alone. We've got each other, and we have plenty of food and plenty of fun things to do. So don't worry."

"Well, if you're sure you're alright."

"I am."

"Well, I'll be up here prayin', and as soon as the water goes down I'll be home. Call me if you want to talk about anything, okay?"

I really wanted to ask her who this mystery kid was in all the pictures. But that would have to wait for another day.

"Okay. Love you, Mamaw."

"Love you too, my dear girl. Go eat some cookies and I'll see you soon."

I hung up the phone and grabbed a snickerdoodle. I looked over at my cousins, hunched over the photo albums, and felt a wave of gratefulness for each one—unique and annoying as they can all be at times.

Hunter's gonna love being a Carroway.

Before I could even finish thinking that thought, panic gripped me, and I almost choked on my cookie.

"What time is it?" I grabbed my phone, only to find out it had died, probably drained from searching for service. I ran to look at the battery-powered clock on the family room wall.

"What time did we leave Hunter in the shed? Has it been an hour yet?"

The girls' heads popped up from their books. Lola's eyes bugged out and she grabbed her throat.

"I set a timer on my phone when we left him." She ran over to check it. "It's been eighty minutes!"

"Oh, no!" Ruby ran toward the mudroom. "How could we forget about Hunter? I hope he's okay!"

We dropped everything we were doing and followed Ruby to the mudroom. In seconds, we were in our raincoats and boots again, and it didn't even matter that it was pouring extra hard—we ran like cheetahs up toward the shed.

CHAPTER 25

The Big Reveal

Hunter!" Kendall used her concert voice when we got to the opened door of the shed. "Hunter! You passed the challenge! You can come on out now!"

We stood and waited. But there was no answer.

"HUNTER!"

Nothing.

I pushed Kendall out of the way and shined my headlamp into the shed. I moved the beam left and right, up and down, but all I saw were stuffed heads, rusty tools, and boxes of junk.

No Hunter.

Ruby pushed me aside.

"I'm goin' in."

Ruby disappeared inside. And when she didn't come back right away, I went in too.

"Hunter? Are you in here?"

My voice echoed, startling me, and I backed up, right into Kendall.

"Ouch," Kendall said. "Your head hit me in the chin."

"Sorry."

"Is h-he in there?" Lola spoke from the entrance. She was either freezing or scared. Probably both.

"I don't see him anywhere. Hunter!" Ruby continued to

shine her light in all the corners, and she even began opening boxes. "Maybe he's hiding to give us a scare."

"Well, it's working," Lola said.

"Hunter Carroway, you come out here right now!" Even Kendall began opening boxes now.

I shined my headlamp in all directions.

"People, let's face it. He's not in here."

Lola started crying. "I knew we shouldn't have sent him in here with that gator! How could we be so mean! He never stood a chance! Now he's not going to be our cous—"

I ran over toward Lola and grabbed her shoulders.

"Stop, Lola. Just stop." Then I turned back around. "Hunter is okay, I know it. We'll find him. It won't do us any good to panic right now!"

"We gotta get outta here before the gator comes back." Lola turned and ran toward the barn.

"We need a plan," Ruby said to me. "Where should we look? Just about every place is under water right now."

"Let's get the kayak," I said. "It's only been a few minutes over an hour. He couldn't have gone very far."

I suddenly remembered something and went back into the shed.

I shined my light all around. The slingshot was missing.

"Girls, I think I know what's going on here. Hunter is out working on challenge two. If we can find some squirrels, I bet we'll find him."

"I hope you're right," Kendall said.

"I know I'm right."

We ran down the hill to catch up with Lola, and then we

slowed a little, all the while calling Hunter's name. But the only answer that came was a crackle of thunder.

"I don't think we should be out here," Lola said.

I know I'm not supposed to be out here.

"He's not on this hill anywhere," Ruby said. "Are you sure the kayak is going to float with all four of us in it?"

"I was out on it last week with my dad and a bunch of gear," I said. "That thing's solid."

When we got to the house, we climbed up the stairs to the porch and muscled the kayak down. We carried it to the prayer bench, hooked up the seats, and Ruby and Lola jumped in.

Kendall walked up and linked her arm with mine.

"Are we really doin' this?" she said.

"Yes, we are. We're Carroways, and we can handle anything with God's help. Right?"

Kendall smiled. "Right."

Kendall helped me shove the kayak into the water. We waded in and, despite an uncoordinated couple of seconds where I tripped over my feet and landed on my knees in the water, we managed to hoist ourselves in and join Lola and Ruby.

Ruby and Kendall grabbed the two paddles and sat at opposite ends of the kayak, with Kendall in the front.

I pointed north. "Let's go toward Aunt Janelle's. Every time I've been out hiking with Hunter, we've gone that way. Stay near the shore."

"The shore? This isn't normally the shore. It's Mamaw and Papaw's front yard." Ruby stood and pushed her paddle down into the water. "It's about three feet deep right here. Wow!"

"Okay, then just go that way, toward the slough." I squinted into the dark night, in the direction of the swampy arm of the

river that we normally avoid because of the possibility of running into disgusting critters. "He might have gone there to look for that frog or something to hunt."

The rain was still coming down, but it wasn't pouring anymore. Still, I pulled my hood up over my eyes so the water wouldn't blur my vision. The headlamp beam was weak, so I needed all the help I could get.

"HUNTER!" Kendall cupped her hands around her mouth and yelled with all of her amazing lung strength.

"Hunter!" Lola tried, but I could barely hear her. I think she was still crying.

We paddled downriver for a couple of minutes, maneuvering around trees that were quickly disappearing because of the rising river. The current moved much faster than I expected. Sticks, leaves, and other junk that had washed down the hills into the river scraped the sides of our kayak as it floated by.

"Ruby and Kendall, paddle backward so we'll slow down. If he's out here we don't want to float by him."

"If he's out here?" Kendall swung her head back to look at me. "If?"

"Hunter!" Ruby yelled from the back while back-paddling with all her might.

I tried to yell. "Hunt—" but then I had to stop. All of a sudden my lungs were fighting me.

"What's that?" Kendall pointed to the right bank, close to where the slough usually joins the river. It was hard to tell with the water so high. I glanced that way, and I thought I saw movement near where the water swirled around a couple of trees in front of a flooded gazebo. I pointed my headlamp and tried to take a deep breath to yell Hunter's name. Thankfully, Kendall yelled first.

"Hunter!"

A voice came out of the trees.

"Over here!"

It was him alright.

"Ruby, paddle forward now, but just with your left paddle. We need to get over near those trees." I pointed over to where I thought Hunter was.

"Hunter, stop moving! We're coming for you!" It took about all the energy I had to shout.

Lola brought her headlamp out and shined it in Hunter's direction. The light caught some reflective strips on his raincoat, and now I could see his teeth. What was that boy doing smiling in the middle of this flood?

"Paddle harder, Ruby!" Kendall dug in harder. "We're almost there!"

"I'll jump out when we get close to land and drag us in," I said. "Kendall, give me your headlamp. I can barely see him." Kendall reached back with her light, and I leaned forward to grab it. I pushed my hood off and strapped mine onto my head and held Kendall's with my hand, hoping to shine more light in the same direction. "We can't pass him!"

"Girls! Over here!" Hunter came into clearer view now. He was crawling along what was the new bank of the river and reaching into the water.

"You're gonna get swept in!" Kendall yelled. "Move back, Hunter!"

Right about then, our kayak hit a tree stump, and the rushing current turned us backward and beached us near the first tree by the gazebo.

"Grab the boat and drag it up on the dirt so we don't lose

it!" I jumped out of the kayak, fought my way through some low hanging tree branches, and ran toward Hunter.

"Hunter! We're here with a boat. Come on back here!"

"Allie! I found your backpack! It's caught around a frog's neck!" Hunter leaped forward a couple of feet downriver. "I almost have him!"

"Leave it! You're going to fall into the river!" I stepped forward and tripped over a stick, landing on my hands and knees in the spongy swamp. I looked back, realizing it wasn't a stick. It was Hunter's slingshot.

"He keeps hopping toward me and then away. I'll have him in just a couple of minutes!"

"Hunter! This is really dangerous! Come back!" Kendall ran in front of me and kicked mud up behind her which splattered on my face. Ruby and Lola passed me too. Lola picked up the slingshot.

My lungs were giving me the fight of my life. I tried to get up, and I took a few steps, but then I stopped, bent over, and coughed as hard as I could. I breathed in and . . . nothing.

I put my hand out and squeaked. "Guys . . . wait . . . up!" But they were too far ahead. Hunter kept hopping, forward then back. I prayed he would catch that frog so I could use my inhaler in a couple of minutes. I resolved to keep moving forward. One step. Two steps. Three.

I finally caught up.

There they sat, at the side of the river, all my cousins, drenched, muddy . . . and laughing.

"He did it!" Though rain was running into her eyes, Ruby was smiling. "He completed challenge one! This is definitely the frog that got away. I can tell by his beefy legs."

She held up Mr. Bullfrog. Then she kissed it. Disgusting.

Hunter held up my pink Allie-Kit.

"He tried to get away with this, but I wouldn't let him."

I sat down and worked to catch a breath.

"Thanks, Hunter."

I reached for the backpack and tried to open it to get to the inhaler, but the zipper was stuck. Or my fingers were frozen.

"Why did you leave the shed?" Kendall pushed her brother in the side of the arm. "You scared us half to death."

Hunter looked confused. "The hour was up, and you didn't come back, so I headed back down to the house. It was cold in that shed, you know! But then I saw this pink thing hopping around, and I realized it was Allie's medical kit that she lost, so I followed it. I didn't realize the river was up so high though, so I had to swim a little."

Hunter poked at the frog that Ruby was holding and it croaked. Everyone laughed but me. I was still trying to conserve air and unzip the dumb backpack.

Lola handed Hunter the slingshot. "We thought you went out hunting for squirrels so you could pass challenge two."

Hunter smiled. "That would have been a good idea too. But I can't believe any animals would still be out in this mess."

"*We* need to get out of this mess," Lola said.

"We brought the kayak," Kendall said, and pointed back upriver to the boat, which now had to be about a hundred yards away.

"I hope it's still there," Lola said.

Kendall stood up and tried to brush some mud off her pants.

"Ruby, let that dumb frog go and let's get outta here."

160

Ruby kissed the frog again. "I'm gonna miss you, little troublemaker." She got up and walked a little way to let him go in a shallow area of the river by some trees where the slough comes in.

Then she screamed.

CHAPTER 26

Reptile Wrestling

It was a blood-curdling scream. Nothing like I've ever heard before from Ruby. We all jumped to our feet and bolted toward the river.

Lola got to the riverbank first.

"Ruby! What's wrong?"

Ruby screamed again. She was backed up against a tree.

"It's a gator! He's coming at me! Help!"

Kendall got there next.

"Gator!" Kendall cried.

"Oh no, you CANNOT have MY SISTER!" Lola reached for a loose branch on the ground and began smacking the water near the gator's tail.

Ruby inched her way around the tree trunk but slipped and fell into the swollen river. She coughed and sputtered and backed away from the gator, but it moved forward and snapped its jaws. Ruby squealed and thrashed in the moving current. "He has my coat!" She pulled herself backward, twisting and turning to try to free herself from her raincoat.

"Let . . . me . . . go!"

"He's gonna drown her! Somebody do something!' Lola's cry was a mixture of anger and sobs.

"Jesus, help us!" Kendall grabbed a rock and threw it at the gator's back.

Everything seemed to move in slow motion. Hunter and I ran side-by-side, down the bank, behind the girls. That is, until I ran out of air and fell to the ground. I had nothing left. All I could do now was pray and hope this nightmare would all end soon.

"Lola and Kendall! Move outta the way—I'm comin' through!"

I looked up at that moment and I'll never forget what I saw. There was my new cousin, running strong and confident toward the back of the gator. With the roll of duct tape in his hand.

Could this really be happening?

Hunter picked up speed and let out a warrior yell.

Lord, please help him!

I watched as he dove headfirst, over the tail and on to the gator's back.

Kendall screamed, "Nooooo!"

God, rescue us!

I heard a ripping sound. Hunter's feet kicked, and he and the gator thrashed around in the river.

Thunder cracked.

And then everything went black.

CHAPTER 27

Bayou Blackout

"A llie. Wake up. Come on. I have your inhaler."

It was a familiar voice. Then I felt a sharp pain on my cheek. I opened my eyes. I was on my back, on spongy, wet ground. Thankfully, the rain had stopped.

Hunter was staring me in the face.

"Oh, good. You're awake. Sorry I had to slap you. But I guess it worked."

He grabbed my hands and pulled me up to a sitting position.

"Here." Someone else stuck the inhaler in my mouth. I pulled it out.

"Hold on. I have to blow out first."

"Well, blow out then. You're making me nervous, passing out the way you did."

That was Lola, of course.

I coughed and sputtered but managed to blow out. Then I put the inhaler in my mouth, pressed the button, and breathed in. Held my breath a minute. And spotted Ruby at my side.

I blew back out.

"You survived." I coughed, before reaching out to give her a hug.

"Hunter stopped him, Allie! He taped his mouth shut with the duct tape! It was so scary, I thought he was going to bite Hunter's arm off!"

I craned my neck around to look toward the river.

"Is it gone?"

"The gator? Yeah," Kendall said. "He's gone. And even if it came back, it can't hurt anybody."

"You taped its mouth shut? That's crazy!"

Hunter sat down, took his glasses off, and tried to wipe off the moisture. But every bit of clothing on him was wet.

"Yeah. I saw this guy do it on TV once. If you're on its back, an alligator can't do anything to you, except maybe break your leg with its tail, but I had to take the chance. To save Ruby." He put his glasses back on. "That was really scary!"

I sat there a minute, trying to review the night's events while my lungs cleared. My hands began to shake.

Hunter took off his coat and wrapped it around me.

"We have to get you back to the house, where it's dry and warm. Do you think you can stand up?"

I grabbed my forehead with my hand.

"Let me get this straight. You just wrestled a gator and won?"

"Yes."

"Lola?" I turned to my cousin. "Will you count that as a pass for the hunting challenge? That took a lot more guts than just roasting a squirrel."

Lola wiped tears from her eyes. "Yes. Absolutely. He saved my sister."

"So that means Hunter passed the initiation."

"What? No, I didn't!"

"Hear me out. You had four challenges to complete tonight, right?"

"Right."

"Challenge one: catch five frogs in the mud. You did that. And you caught my backpack too."

"That was so weird how it was stuck on—"

I continued. "Challenge two: hunt something and then cook it."

Lola interrupted. "I say he doesn't have to cook the gator." She looked around at our group. "Is everyone good with that?"

"Yes," Ruby said. "I never want to see *that* alligator again, not even on a plate with horseradish."

"Disgusting," I said. "Okay then." I glanced over at Kendall. "Challenge three was to sing with our quartet and sound good. Hunter, I feel like you did that—and more—but Kendall is the final judge."

We all looked at Kendall.

She closed her eyes and shook her head. "Y'all know what this means, right? Because we know Hunter passed the haunted shed challenge too. If I say yes, the Diva's history."

"Sometimes change is a good thing," I said.

Kendall crossed her arms and rolled her eyes. She didn't say anything for a few moments, and it started to rain again.

"Kendall, we're gonna be washed away in a flash flood if you don't respond soon." Lola pulled her beanie down over her eyes.

"Okay! He passed." Kendall went over and pulled Lola's beanie back up. "I just hope you're ready to do some creative redecorating."

"We can rebuild it and make it better than ever. For everybody." Hunter grinned. "I already talked to Mr. Dimple about helping us with the design."

"Mr. Dimple?" I said. "Did you talk to him today at the burger place?"

"Yes! He's an inventive genius, you know."

"You were *that* confident that you would pass our initiation, huh?" Kendall pushed her brother over in the mud.

"Hey!" He stood up and held up his hands. "Man, I hate this stuff."

"Then let's get out of it, people."

I pushed myself up, relieved to be breathing better, though I was still a jittery mess.

We all started back to the kayak. Hunter picked up his slingshot but then called me back.

"Hey! Don't forget your backpack." Hunter grabbed my kit, which I had left lying in the mud, and latched it onto my wrist. "We don't want to have to chase it back down the river again."

I smiled. "Thanks."

CHAPTER 28

Mamaw's Return

"Wake up, Grands! I've got breakfast for y'all!"

I cracked my eyes open but then closed them again when Mamaw pulled up the window shades in the family room and the bright sunshine blasted me in the face.

"Why are y'all sleepin' out here when we have perfectly good beds in the other room?"

Ruby jumped up off her blanket pile on the floor.

"Mamaw, you're safe!"

"We were so worried," Lola said as she pushed up the recliner and sat up from where she was sleeping. "We've never seen the water up that high."

Mamaw brushed the comment off with her hand.

"That flood last night? It wasn't anything. Before you kids were born, we had a flood that came right up to the porch. Luckily, we had a blowup boat in this very room so we could escape. We paddled for miles to find dry ground."

"Are you serious?" I sat up, stretched, and yawned. "Or is that just another exaggerated Carroway story?"

"Exaggerated? Our family never exaggerates! Now come on over and get some French toast. Y'all must be starvin'!"

Kendall climbed her way out of Papaw's chair in the corner. She stretched her neck back and forth.

"For the record, that chair may look comfy, but it's NOT."

I pulled my feet off the sofa and almost kicked Hunter—who was still sleeping on the floor—in the head.

"Hunter," I nudged him with my hand. "Wake up. Do you want breakfast?"

Hunter opened his eyes and got a big grin on his face.

"Are the lights back on?"

"It's hard to tell with the sun blasting, but I think so. Mamaw's here, and she's cooking."

"She's back?" Hunter pushed his way out of his sleeping bag and ran into the kitchen to hug Mamaw.

"I'm so glad you aren't hurt," he said.

Mamaw hugged him back. "Sweet boy, your Mamaw's tough. I've lived in the bayou a long time. Not much can bring me down." She pulled back from the hug and looked Hunter in the eyes. "Are you okay? Were y'all starved and bored out of your minds last night?"

Lola choke-laughed but then caught herself. "No, we certainly weren't bored. Not one bit."

Mamaw sighed. "Oh, good. When the lights and phones went out I was wonderin' what you were all gonna do without your electronic devices."

"We're Carroways," Hunter said. "We create our own entertainment." Then he did a little beatbox sound and we all laughed.

Mamaw pulled a huge platter of French toast out of the oven and placed it on the island, along with some paper plates, syrup, and butter.

"Eat up," she said. "Papaw might be needing your help with some cleanup today when he finally gets home."

"Oh, no. More mud." Hunter's distressed sigh caused us all to laugh again.

"Yeah, it's a muddy mess out there," Mamaw said. "And speakin' of messes . . ."

She walked over to the side kitchen counter and picked up a couple of photo albums. "What were y'all doin' with the family albums, takin' all these pictures out and leavin' 'em on the island?"

Oh, boy. Here we go.

"We were just curious about our family history," I said.

"Like where I got my red hair," Ruby added.

"And what our dads used to do when they were younger," Kendall said.

"Same things they do now." Mamaw went to the refrigerator, pulled out pitchers of iced tea and orange juice, and placed them on the island. "Hunter, can you get some cups out?"

Hunter did.

And then I decided to wade into some muddy waters.

"We were looking at all those family reunion pictures. There sure were a lot of boys in the family back then."

Mamaw chuckled. "And isn't it *much* better now with all the girls?"

"Hey! What's wrong with boys?" Hunter shoved a big forkful of French toast in his mouth.

"Nothin' at all, darlin'. And you, my boy, are extra-special! It's just I was so outnumbered back then. I couldn't wait for one of my sons to finally get married so I could go shoppin' with someone who didn't want to buy just fishin' gear."

Mamaw went back to the stack of photos and picked up the one on the top of the stack. She wrinkled up her forehead, and her voice turned stern.

"Where did *this* come from?"

She turned the picture around so we could see the mystery boy standing next to the cornucopia tent.

No one said anything.

I swallowed my French toast bite, took a swig of tea, and cleared my throat.

"We were wondering the same thing. He has red hair like Ruby, so she thought maybe he's a family member we haven't met." I walked over to the stack and picked up the family reunion picture. "He's in this picture too, with you and Papaw and our dads, I think."

Mamaw moved over next to me and stared at the picture.

"That little rascal . . ."

Hunter just kept chewing away, oblivious to the mystery that—I hoped—was about to be solved. We girls all focused our gaze on Mamaw, who looked like she was getting a little grumpy.

"That boy . . ."

She stomped across the room to get a tissue.

Maybe she's not grumpy, maybe she's sad.

"That boy was the only human on earth . . ."

She wiped her nose.

What? What? What?

Mamaw shook her head. "Why aren't y'all eatin'? Is somethin' wrong with the French toast?"

"Nothing's wrong," Ruby said. "We just can't wait to hear who the boy is."

Mamaw pulled up a stool. We all leaned in. Well, all except Hunter, who was finishing up the pile of French toast.

Mamaw sat down and rested her chin on her clasped hands.

"That boy's name is Andrew Doonsberry. He lived just up

the river, but you'd think he lived at our house, since he was here *all* the time—driving me nuts, sneakin' his face into our family pictures. I called him 'Doomsberry,' because every time he was around, there was trouble." Mamaw pointed at the picture. "You see this photo? It makes my blood boil! That tent is made out of my favorite Thanksgiving tablecloth. The rascal stole it out of my storage shed! He took 'em all—Christmas, Valentine's, Easter—and made tents, blankets, and knapsacks out of 'em! Those tablecloths were heirlooms passed down from my Great Mamaw Emily. He denied it, of course, but look at that tent! It's got a cornucopia on it!"

Now even Hunter was fully engaged in the story.

"Are you talking about the haunted shed? The one up the hill from here? By the barn?" Hunter looked at me and wiggled his eyebrows up and down.

Mamaw shook her head and hid her face in her hands for a minute. "It's not haunted. Your dads and I started that rumor to try to keep Andy from goin' in there to steal more of my stuff."

Andy.

Mamaw looked up and put her hand to her heart.

"We even started a story—that there was a demon alligator in the shed who ate twelve-year-old boys. One day, your dads took Andy up to the shed, made a bunch of groanin' sounds, and knocked over a bunch of boxes. Then they told him that the gator ate . . . your dad, I think." Mamaw pointed to Kendall. "He would have been about twelve at the time."

"Wow. That must have been scary," Hunter said.

All of a sudden, Mamaw looked sad.

"It was. In fact, we never saw Andy again after that day. I had to ask God to forgive me. He was the only human on earth who I had trouble forgiving, and I promised that if he ever came back, I would do my best to try to really love him."

Romans 12. Where Mamaw wrote Andy's name.

Mamaw's face brightened a bit.

"It was so bad that I couldn't bring myself to buy another tablecloth. Ever." She looked up at us. "I suppose that sounds silly to all of you, right?"

"Not really," Ruby said. She put her hand on Mamaw's. "I always thought you just loved placemats better."

Mamaw patted Ruby on the shoulder. "Well, I'm glad I was able to clear up the mystery for you."

You have no idea.

Papaw came in through the kitchen door just then, and walked over to the cupboard to grab a plate. "What are all y'all doin' in here eatin' when there's shovelin' to be done?" He walked around the island and sniffed. "The problem here is I smell the best French toast in the world, but I don't see any. Hunter, did you eat it all?"

Mamaw went over and gave Papaw a hug.

"I'll make you all you want. I'm just glad you're back safe."

"How was the sleepover with the grandkids?"

Mamaw laughed. "I wasn't here. You'll have to ask them."

CHAPTER 29

For Sale

Uncle Wayne drove his big truck out to Mamaw's house and brought us all home that afternoon.

"How did y'all like the flood? You know, one time the water came all the way . . ."

"Up to the porch," we said in unison.

"Oh, you heard that story?"

"A few times," I said.

Uncle Wayne nodded. "Well, it's a classic." He pulled into our driveway and pointed to a new sign in our front yard. "Hey! Check that out!"

It was the most horrific sight ever.

For Sale.

Bayou's Best Realty.

Tears filled my eyes. I covered them with the sleeves of my hoodie.

Lola leaned over and whispered in my ear, "I knew it." She put her arm around me. "I don't want you to go."

"Tell that to my parents."

Uncle Wayne got out of the truck and grabbed my bag out of the back.

I jumped out of the side door and stood in the driveway. For a split second, I considered taking off and running back to Mamaw's. A pace that didn't change.

I took my bag from Uncle Wayne.

"Did you know anything about this?" I asked him and tipped my head toward the sign.

He shrugged. "I know your parents have been considering selling the house. Guess they decided to pull the trigger. Kind of exciting if you ask me."

Sure. If you call cactus exciting.

The garage door was open, and unfortunately, both my parent's vehicles were there. Uncle Wayne jumped into his truck, put it in reverse, and inched backward. "See ya, Allie."

The back driver's side window slid down, and Ruby stuck her head out.

"Text us! We'll meet in the Diva and come up with a plan. I'll bring cookies."

I worked up a small smile and waved goodbye. My cousins waved back. I imagined the day that I would be in our car, pulling out, waving goodbye . . . for good.

I stood there, in the driveway, all alone. A few drops of rain started to fall on my cheeks. Good. If I was mostly wet when I walked in, no one would suspect I'd been crying. I thought about running again, trying to disappear where nobody would find me, but then I realized that was the opposite of what I really wanted to do. I wanted to stay in this place. Forever. With the people I love.

"God, help me to know what to do right now. I feel like throwing a temper tantrum, possibly taking an axe to that sign. But would that really help anything?"

Go inside, Allie. Change is a good thing, you'll see. Your parents love you

This was another time it was going to be hard to obey that voice. But I did, after I went over and kicked the sign.

"Allie?" Mom called out to me from the sofa, where she was sitting next to my dad, watching a movie. Dad pushed pause on the remote.

"Well, it sounds like you kids had a little more than you bargained for during that sleepover. Come on over and tell us about it!" Dad scooted over, leaving me room to sit in the middle of the very people I was mad at right now.

I put my bag down and stepped in a few feet.

"I'm wet. I should go change."

"Nonsense." Dad waved me over. "We can handle a little water. It'll add some special effects to your story."

It was clear I wasn't getting out of this. I dropped my bag on the floor and made my way over to sit in the gap between my parents.

"We're so glad you're safe," Mom said. Then they both reached over to hug me and kiss me on the cheeks.

I put my arms out. "Okay, okay! I have asthma, people, remember? Give a poor kid some air."

Mom laughed and pulled back.

"Speaking of that," she said. "Did you have to use your inhaler last night?"

"Oh, yeah," I said. "It was tons of fun. I huffed and puffed like the big, bad wolf."

"And did it work?" Her eyes searched mine, and I looked away so she wouldn't see the pain and anger.

I crossed my arms. "Yes, ma'am. It cleared my lungs up right away, but it made my hands shake. It was kinda freaky, actually."

"Well, as long as it worked," Dad said.

"Hey," Mom said, and she patted me on the knee. "We have a surprise for you." I couldn't hold the frustration in anymore.

"Does it have to do with the for sale sign that's out in front of the house?"

Mom's eyes opened wide.

"What? There's a sign?" She turned to my dad. "Jake?"

Dad jumped up off the couch and ran out the front door. He returned in seconds.

"Yep, there's a sign out there. I can't believe they put it up already."

"Well," I said, "that's what you get when you hire Bayou's Best Realty."

"Oh, dear. We had planned to talk to you about it first, Allie. Some things are about to change around here." Mom was smiling, and I was struck with a little déjà vu since that was the exact same wording she used when she told me that Hunter was going to be adopted.

I gripped the couch cushion tight.

You can handle this, Allie. Whatever it is.

"Are we moving into the Joshua model? Should I start reading up on how to grow cactus? Or are we moving to Timbuktu?"

"Well," Dad chuckled a little and stroked his beard. "As a matter of fact . . . we are moving to Timbuktu."

My stomach did a flip and I think it landed in my throat.

"Dad, that's in Siberia or something. You can't be serious."

He pointed his index finger in the air. "I beg to differ! Timbuktu is right around the corner."

I looked over at Mom, who was beaming. "Come with us." She reached her hand out to lift me off the couch, and I followed my parents out the front door. It was still drizzling, which is nothing for Louisianans.

We walked past the for sale sign, and the plastic container, which held informational brochures about our house. A smiling Ellen was pictured at the bottom—still wearing the butter-colored suit.

We continued out of our front yard and across the street, over one small hill, until we came to a large empty lot near Kendall's house.

"Allie Kate Carroway—my princess daughter," Dad said, "you are standin' on what will soon be a brand-new cul-de-sac in the neighborhood. Welcome to Timbuktu Court." Dad put his hands out and turned in a complete circle. "I'm kinda proud of the name. I picked it myself."

I looked around. At dirt. I scratched my head.

"Huh?"

"We're building a new house! Isn't that great?" Mom punched her fists in the air and cheered. I half expected her to bust out a cartwheel or two.

"A new house? For *us* to live in?" A few butterflies started to fly around in my gut, but I tried to ignore them while I pulled in a bit more information.

"Well, who else do you think we'd build a house for?" Dad put his hands on his hips.

"Allie," Mom said, "we decided that instead of trying to mold-proof our old home, we'd build a new one—with beautiful new flooring and materials that won't add to your allergy problems."

Everything finally made sense, and I felt the dark cloud that had been hanging around my heart disappear, leaving room for some hope and light once again. I flew into Mom's arms, and then the sobs came.

"Honey, what's wrong?"

I shook my head. "Nothing. Thank you. Thank you so much." Then I just cried for what seemed like an hour.

You were right, God. You had this under control the whole time. I don't know why I ever doubted you.

Dad came over and joined our hug. "We don't really know the timeframe yet, but we decided to put the house up for sale now since it's a slow time in the market. If we do sell the house before the new one is built, we might have to move in with the cousins for a while. That's the bad news."

I pulled my face away from Mom's soaked shirt, sniffed, and wiped my nose with my sleeve. "Bad news? I thought we were moving hundreds of miles *away* from the cousins. Living with them instead is the best news ever!"

"Ha!" Dad bent over laughing. "You just keep telling yourself that."

"I will, Dad. And thank you." Then I hugged him.

"I love you, Allie. I told you I would do anything to rescue you. And I always keep my word, which is why we're moving to Timbuktu Court—lickety split."

CHAPTER 30

Duck Blind Dedication

A week later was Hunter's "official" adoption day. And as I predicted, it was pretty boring for us kids, with lots of standing around at the courthouse, paper signing, and family photo sessions. We filmed a little, too, for an episode of *Carried Away with the Carroways*.

"My collar is scratching me!" Hunter pulled his stiff white dress shirt collar and green tie away from his neck. "How come it's so hot today?"

We all stood there, on the steps of the courthouse, pulling our clothes away from our hot skin.

"Are we done filming yet?" Ruby asked, as she pushed her lacy green dress sleeves up past her elbows. "Where's Hannah? I need to ask her if I can change into my T-shirt and jeans."

"Me too," I said. "Hey, don't you people forget, we have the new duck blind dedication later. And you can wear whatever you want."

"I can't wait," Hunter said. "I think after that I'll finally be able to call myself a real Carroway."

"Hunter, you've been a real Carroway this whole time! You were a Carroway before we even met you. God planned it, you know." I lightly punched him in the arm.

Hunter smiled. "Yeah, I guess you're right. I did feel like we had a bond from the first day we all met. And then, during the flood, when all that crazy stuff was happening and you were all in danger, I just knew in my heart, that no matter if I got lost, or hurt, or if I had to do something uncomfortable to rescue one of you, I'd do it. No question. Because you're my family. Lickety split, I'd be there for any of you."

I froze on the steps. "Wait, Hunter. What did you just say?"

"I said I would be there for you. You're family."

"No, before that."

"Lickety split?" Hunter smiled. "Oh, that's just a saying that means super-fast."

"I know what it means. My dad says it all the time."

"Ours does too," Lola added.

"And ours." Kendall put her arm around her new brother.

"Well," I said, "it sounds like a Carroway thing. What do you think about naming our new duck blind 'The Lickety Split?'"

Ruby gasped. "It's perfect! And think about this! Remember when that alligator had a hold of my coat?

Lola shuddered. "How can we forget?"

Ruby continued, "And Kendall cried out to Jesus for help?"

Kendall grimaced. "Yeah, I guess I sorta screamed a little bit."

"I was praying too," I said, "while I was laying there in the mud, being no help at all."

"What about me?" Hunter said. "You better believe I was praying when I dove on the gator's back."

"And I was crying," Lola said, "and praying that I wouldn't lose my sister."

"Well, then," Ruby said, "I'd say God certainly rescued us, lickety split, wouldn't you?"

"I guess that settles it." I crossed my arms and nodded.

"We'll see you this afternoon for the dedication of The Lickety Split."

It was the most amazing day ever. I arrived early for the dedication, and as I climbed the pink-and-purple painted wooden steps, I wondered what the new colors would be. Or if we would even have these steps in the new duck blind design. I entered our girl-haven, raised the awnings to let in the late afternoon sun, and plunked down in the turquoise glitter beanbag for possibly the last time.

God, thank you for speaking to me about changing this place to honor Hunter. It wasn't easy to obey, but I know it was the right thing to do. You're awesome, God.

"California, here I come!"

"Little Red!"

"Doe, a dear, a female dear!"

I jumped up and poked my head out the window.

"You're all here on time? Together? This is a first!"

"I brought homemade cookies." Ruby held up a basket.

"Well, get up here!"

I heard the squeak of the gate and seconds later, all the girl cousins were sitting in their regular girly places.

"Hey, Allie, how come you never say your password, huh?" Kendall had her hands glued to the straps of her messenger bag.

"Uh, probably because I'm always here first? So I'm kinda like the gatekeeper?"

"What *is* your password? I don't even remember." Lola raked her fingers through her shiny bob that looked like it had a new, darker-shade-of-pink streak.

"It's Allie-gator."

"Oh, yeah," Ruby said. "Seems like you should change that, given the events of the past week."

"Yes," I said. "Change seems to be a good thing these days."

Just then, a gummi frog came flying through the window. This time, it didn't hit anything. It just shot in one window and out the other side.

Kendall poked her head out the window. "That will be enough frogs for now, Brother."

"Oh, good. You're there!" Hunter yelled. "Just checking. I'm here with my password … Gator Buster! And I don't want to change it."

"Sounds perfect," I said, "given the events of the past week. Come on up!"

Hunter squeaked through the gate, ran up the stairs, and entered the blind, carrying his bucket of candy frogs and a cardboard tube clamped between his arm and torso. "I got the plans from Mr. Dimple at the courthouse. Wait till you see what The Lickety Split is going to look like!"

He popped the plastic cap off one end and started to shake the rolled-up plans out of the tube, but I put my hand out to stop him.

"Not yet. First we have to do the dedication. Have a seat."

I gestured to a place next to me on the turquoise beans.

"Sorry about the girly furniture. You'll have to endure it one last time."

"I consider it an honor," Hunter said, and then he plunked down.

I stood up and pulled my prepared speech out of my tote bag. I unfolded the paper, pulled it tight between my hands, and took a deep breath, which came easily thanks to the new inhaler.

I cleared my throat and began.

"To all Carroway Cousins, far and near; to those we know about, and to those whom God may add in the future through birth, adoption, or other creative means—this place is for you. The Bible says this in Romans 12 'Don't just pretend to love others. Really love them. Hate what is wrong. Hold tightly to what is good. Love each other with genuine affection, and take delight in honoring each other.'

"Keeping this in mind, we hereby dedicate our new future duck blind—The Lickety Split—for the purpose of honoring each other. We are all God's children. Unique and special. And it doesn't matter if you're a boy or a girl, a singer or a hunter, or whether you are allergic to peanuts or mud, you are always welcome here."

I looked up at my cousins. Lola was sniffling, but everyone else just had a little grin on their face. I folded up the paper.

"And no more passwords are needed," I said.

The response was thunderous applause.

"That was beautiful, Allie." Lola pulled a tissue out of the purple crocheted box on the teacart.

"Thanks. There's a place for us all to sign and date at the bottom. Then we'll frame it and put it at the entrance when The Lickety Split is finished."

"Ooh, this is just like the Declaration of Independence." Hunter was the first one to sign, his signature taking up most of the room on the page, just like John Hancock. We all did our best to squeeze our signatures around his, and then we stood around eating Ruby's delicious cookies.

"I think we should wait to look at the plans," Hunter said. "You girls might need a little time to prepare your minds. Mr. Dimple said this place is a dump, and it should all come down. Except the tree, of course."

"Good idea, Hunter," I said. "Why don't you bring them to my house Sunday after church, and we'll spread them out on our big round table."

"Can we at least take down some of our stuff?" Ruby asked. "I want to keep my Bible verses."

"Sure. We have time." I pulled the big beanbag to the center of the room. "We can stack it all on here and bring up some boxes later to pack it all up."

"Ruby and Lola," Kendall said, "you can take the teapot clock, since there are two of you in the same house to enjoy it."

Lola, who happened to be hugging the clock at that moment, smiled. "Thanks."

"Someone needs to make these awful glitter ducks disappear," Hunter said.

"I will," Kendall said, and she pulled them down from the hook on the ceiling. "They are a little over the top, I guess."

I walked over to my Allie wall.

"Hunter, can I hand these boards to you?" I tried to pull the one off the wall that had the verse from 2 Corinthians. The one about being a new creation. It didn't budge, so I applied a little pressure, pushing it from side to side, to loosen the nails. Finally, it came off.

"Ewww, what *is* that?" Hunter moved toward the black goo

that was left on the wall after I pulled the board off. He pushed his finger in, sniffed it, and pulled back.

"Get away, Allie!" Hunter turned and pushed me near the entrance to the blind.

"What's wrong, Hunter? What is that stuff?"

"I'll tell you what it is. It's mold! And I'm pretty sure it's a bad kind. I knew this place smelled weird."

At that same time, Kendall and Lola pulled boards off their walls.

"Yucko! It's over here too!" Kendall grabbed her throat and stepped back from the wall. "Allie, you need to get out of here right now."

"We should all get out," Hunter said. "This place is a biohazard. Allie, no wonder you can never breathe in here."

I felt the blood drain from my face. What had Dr. Snow said? That I was overloaded with allergens, like a glass of water, filled to the brim and ready to spill over. Lately, I had been spending a lot of time in the Diva—sometimes even leaning my head against those moldy boards!

And every time I left, I had an asthma attack!

The Diva had been making me sick all this time . . . and God knew it.

Could this be another reason that you told me the Diva had to go? Wow, God.

"Well, come on, let's go. We don't want to have to drag you out of here coughing and sputtering." Kendall grabbed me by the arm and pulled me down the steps of the Diva. "I'll come back later and pack up. Your days in that mold castle are over, princess."

Princess.

I've never liked that term, probably because it makes me think of ruffly dresses and tiaras, which aren't really my style. But now, from where I sat there with my cousins, looking up at the Diva from the old wooden bench, I gained a new perspective:

My God is the King of Kings, and I am his valued daughter. A princess! I'm a girl that God chose to be in his family, a girl that he knows everything about, and a girl that he cared enough about to rescue, so I can live a life that will bring honor to him. Being a princess doesn't have anything to do with where I live, what my talents are, what I'm allergic to, or what I wear.

I took a deep breath, and I never felt so grateful for it in my entire life. I closed my eyes and raised my face to the sun.

Thank you, God. For loving me.

Your Princess in Camo.

Running from Reality

Allie Carroway is done. With reality TV that is. It seemed fun at first, to be part of a famous family, but life gets embarrassing and challenging especially when every detail of your life is filmed for the world to see. Allie's cousins, Kendall, Ruby, Lola, and Hunter have had enough too. Each one has experienced some embarrassment, and lately it seems that all they do is complain about the show and how they don't like having everyone know what is going on in their lives. But when the cousins call a strike, they are quickly reminded that they can't go back on a decision they made as a family.

But Papaw Ray has a surprise for the kids. He sends them on a trip to escape reality. With hunting season and the holidays just around the corner, it's the perfect time to take a trip and escape the show—but on one condition. They can't tell anyone about their adventures, no matter how fun, challenging, or even amazing they are. No cameras or pictures allowed.

Allie, her cousins, and the family head for California and warmer weather, only to find that what's in store will be the hardest secret they've ever had to keep. Especially when what they learn, and the ways God allows them to help others, can give people hope and be light for all to see.

This series explores the nature of a family filled with social, cultural, and physical diversity. In a world splashed with class and camouflage, the cousins are constantly looking for ways to love unconditionally through all the hiccups, with the love and faith of family.

Available in stores and online!

Connect with Faithgirlz!

 http://www.faithgirlz.com/

 www.facebook.com/Faithgirlz/

 www.instagram.com/zonderkidz_faithgirlz/

9–1–1!

The day we filmed the Carroway Family Christmas episode—Friday, October 31st—was the day I ended up in the emergency room with a bunch of sick and injured trick-or-treaters.

The whole scene was weird. A huge, decorated Christmas tree, strung with multicolored lights, stood in the corner of my Aunt Kassie and Uncle Wayne's living room, and stockings—one for each person in our extended family—hung across their massive fireplace mantle. A bowl of Halloween candy sat on a tray by the front door, in case any of the little kids from the neighborhood came early to trick-or-treat. Christmas carols played on the sound system, and all my aunts, uncles, and cousins—dressed in ugly Christmas sweaters—took their assigned seats around three separate dinner tables and filled their mason jar mugs with sparkling cider for our traditional Christmas dinner toast.

It was taking forever for the film crew to set up, and I was starving. So, before I sat down, I snuck into the kitchen and grabbed a Rice Krispy treat from the dessert tray. I hid it in my pants pocket and listened as our director, Zeke, barked instructions.

"Okay, I know it's spooky and Halloween-y out there . . ." Zeke curled up his fingers to look like spider legs.

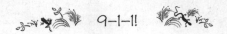

". . . but in here we're all merry and bright!" He smiled big and swung his arms around like a choir conductor. "Got it?"

Most of us laughed, but Kendall, my thirteen-year-old cousin, sighed out loud.

"What-*ever.*"

"Hey—no grinches on the set!" Kendall's dad—my uncle Wayne—threw a napkin ball at her, and it smacked her right in the throat, which was covered by a leather choker. This one had a blue gemstone in the middle of it.

Kendall readjusted her choker and smoothed her straight, shoulder length, light-brown hair.

"Then can we really sing something? That would help me get in the spirit." Kendall loves to sing, and always looks for an opportunity. Lucky for us she's good.

"Not yet," Zeke said. "First we have to eat."

"I'm not hungry." One of my other preteen cousins, Lola, brushed her fingers through the pink streak in her short, dark-brown hair and grimaced at the green bean casserole in front of her. "It may look good, but we kind of know better, right?"

"But this is a new caterer, and I hear the food's delicious." Lola's younger sister, Ruby—who is the best baker I know besides my Mamaw Kat—poked a finger in the green bean goo, licked it, and then smiled.

"I'm willing to give eating a try." Hunter, Kendall's newly adopted twelve-year-old brother sat next to me and rubbed his belly. "I'm starving!" He reached for a roll, and right as he did, a freckled hand appeared from behind and knocked it down.

"Not yet, mister." It was Hannah, our wardrobe manager. Sometimes—okay, lots of times—her duties expand outside the boundaries of just controlling what we wear. She's petite, but she can be scary. And tonight, she had styled her short red bedhead to make her look like a zombie, and had drawn some zipper lips on her face with an eyeliner pencil.

"Here." I broke off half my Krispy treat and discreetly handed it to Hunter under the table.

Hunter smiled, took the treat with one hand, and pushed his rectangular dark-rimmed glasses up on his nose with the other.

"Thanks," he whispered.

He started to lift the treat to his mouth, but stopped when Zeke began directing again.

"Okay, everyone. Here's how this is going down. Papaw Ray will give the toast. Then after you clink your glasses, Wayne will say a prayer. Then Kat'll serve the turkey, and y'all take it from there. Just have a good time, talk, and eat. When we're finished filming your table, we'll let you know."

"I can already tell this turkey isn't as moist as mine." Mamaw Kat used to make the food for all our episodes, but when the producers started scheduling several meal scenes a day, she couldn't keep up. That's when all the caterers in town began competing for the job of feeding the Carroways, and if I had to rank them, they'd all tie for last place.

"The turkey looks fine, Kat." My mom picked up a piece of turkey to inspect it, but then frowned and dropped it in the gravy boat. "There. Now it's moist."

Mamaw laughed. "Well, at least I'm cookin' our real Christmas dinner."

My stomach gurgled right then since my Krispy treat was not filling me up at all. I stood and faced the family. "People— let's get this thing done in one take. I want to hand out candy to the little monsters."